A Regicide

Alain Robbe-Grillet

Translated by John Calder

T0346838

CALDER

CALDER PUBLICATIONS
an imprint of

ALMA BOOKS LTD
3 Castle Yard
Richmond
Surrey TW10 6TF
United Kingdom
www.calderpublications.com

A Regicide first published in French as *Un régicide* by Les Éditions de
Minuit in 1978
This translation first published by Alma Classics in 2015
This new edition first published by Calder Publications in 2018
© Les Éditions de Minuit, 1978
Translation © John Calder, 2015

Cover: Will Dady

Printed and bound by CPI Group (UK) Ltd, Croydon, CR0 4YY

ISBN: 978-0-7145-4859-3

Contents

Translator's Preface

Alain Robbe-Grillet's first novel was published late in France, in 1978, and even later in its English translation, in 2015, seven years after the author's death. The reasons have something to do with my own financial difficulties as a publisher of largely intellectual European modern literature at a time when fashion was changing, mainly due to the arrival of the Thatcher government in the year of French publication, which quickly led to British universities being discouraged from teaching the arts and comparative literature – especially if foreign – and to the emphasis in higher education being switched to business studies and money-making careers. At the same time, Arts Council subsidy, which enabled my publishing company to bring out translations of the best European authors, was terminated, except for a few publishers who made it their business to be seen at Tory Party conferences and show their allegiance to the new regime. It was also one reason why I decided to translate a novel which I much admired, had enjoyed reading and felt could appeal to readers who had found difficulties in Robbe-Grillet's later work, which required some ability to follow clues and solve puzzles.

A Regicide – which, as the author explains in his introduction, did not find a publisher until he was well established with his later novels – does however have the advantage of containing in embryo many of the techniques, preoccupations and innovations that have become familiar to his readers through his other works – the novels from *The Erasers* onwards and his films, of which the best-known remains the first, *Last Year at Marienbad*. In his autobiography, *Ghosts in the Mirror*, a book which could just as well be described as fiction, he describes *A Regicide* as echoing memories, obsessions and locations remembered from his childhood and youth, in particular his recollections of the Brittany coast, which is so well described – but with significant differences as to climate in particular – as Boris's island.

Twice-told tales, or the same tale told differently, are a Robbe-Grillet hallmark. Boris's twin lives do not stretch the imagination as much as the repeated events of his later novels; his blend of seeing life as observation, of the memory of observation, of dream reality, daydream and pure imagination, all stress the richness of the mind through which, and in which, all our lives are lived. What emerges from *A Regicide*, a first novel that is astonishing in its originality and its contrasts, is that there is more of the poet in Robbe-Grillet than his critics and admirers have noticed. There is nothing dry about *A Regicide*, and Boris, a prototypical anti-hero, emerges as a credible character, his life and experiences based on the author's own, partly at the giant factory where he was sent to work in Germany during the Second World War and partly after the war at the Institut National de la Statistique, which he left to start writing this novel. He has said that all his fictions are really about himself, and this must be particularly true of his first literary creation. But *Ghosts in the Mirror* gives a very full account of the circumstances that led to the writing of *A Regicide* and of the places, people, institutions and even myths that make an appearance in it. The reader will find that those sections of *Ghosts in the Mirror* that talk about *A Regicide* are really an enjoyable preface to the novel itself.

Alain Robbe-Grillet belongs to that group of French writers whose works have carried the label "Nouveau Roman", although as a form of fiction it pre-dates the 1950s. Nathalie Sarraute's *Tropisms*, even though it consists of short episodes, falls within the definition. But the Nouveau Roman is really an extension of the French "art" novel. There is a direct progression from Stendhal's romanticism and Balzac's naturalistic novel that becomes a line of descent through Flaubert, Zola, Proust, Gide and the Surrealists, to culminate in the group of writers that includes (by seniority) Nathalie Sarraute, Claude Simon, Marguerite Duras, Alain Robbe-Grillet, Claude Mauriac, Robert Pinget and Michel Butor. Some of them may not outlast the judgement of history in terms of general acceptance, but they are all major literary figures by any definition, and I am sure that Alain Robbe-Grillet will ultimately be seen as a mainstream writer. Throughout his career he became the most public personality of the group, a brilliant speaker, exuding total self-assurance, able to expand on the work of others as well as his own, always with good humour. He always came across as the accomplished man of letters who knew exactly where he would stand in literary history. He was one of the most critically articulate French writers since Zola, controversial, practical, stoically philosophical and – a rarity among French writers – generous to others: many young writers owed their first publication to him.

A Regicide is both an excellent introduction for new readers to a major writer and an enjoyable addition to the canon for those already familiar with his work.

– John Calder, 2015

Author's Introduction

A Regicide is my first novel. Finished in 1949, it was submitted to a major Parisian publisher who, in a pleasant enough way, rejected it. At the time I was working as a research engineer at IFAC (Institut des Fruits et Agrumes Coloniaux). Returning from the West Indies at the beginning of 1951, after a stay given over to the study of certain parasites affecting banana trees (*cercospora musæ* and *cosmopolites sordidus*), I found that my rejected manuscript, after several unsuccessful submissions, had landed on the desk of Les Éditions de Minuit. The firm seemed to be interested. I cut their hesitations short: I would write a second book, I said, and I thought that might make it easier for them to decide. It happened exactly that way: *The Erasers*, finished at the end of 1952, was quickly published. I then thought of bringing out *A Regicide*, a less accessible book. But on rereading it, it seemed to me that the text needed revision. And once again, I preferred to give my time entirely to the new novel which was occupying my mind at the time, *The Voyeur*. The more the time passed, the more changes I found necessary to make to my first work and the less opportune it was to interrupt the flow of the work on which I was currently engaged.

It was only in 1957, after publishing *Jealousy*, that I returned to this work of revision. On the first page I corrected two words, twenty on the second, rather more on the third. From the fifth onward, I totally rewrote the text. At the tenth, I stopped, faced with the whole absurdity of the enterprise; and instead I wrote *In the Labyrinth*. I then decided to give the public the book such as it was, or almost, with only a few changes of punctuation, vocabulary and syntax, perhaps two or three per page. Only one of these changes is important, a change in the name of the hero: Philippe became Boris in 1957. The corrections made that year have in fact been retained here, so that only the fourth to the ninth pages are not the original ones.

– Alain Robbe-Grillet, July 1978

A Regicide

1

I T IS NIGHTFALL AGAIN, and now a stretch of fine sand has to be negotiated along the seashore, broken up by rocks and hollows, with water sometimes up to the waist. The sea is rising, the waves suddenly coming together from many directions and mingling in dangerous eddies. Here and there a smoother surface, covered only by a thin film of liquid, allows a moment of swifter progress; but it is just then that there is a constant risk of losing one's balance in some narrow passage between the rocky walls among the hollows gouged out by the sea; often one has even to retrace one's steps and look for another way forward before the night becomes totally black, but the water rising and growing rougher makes such retreats even more perilous. There is no question of trying to swim in this tumult. Nor can there be any question of hesitating for any length of time as to which is the best way forward. The level of the sea is rising everywhere, the waves are increasing in strength and the power of the currents is growing stronger. But now that any turning back has clearly become impossible, the sand, which rises gently towards the shore, begins to appear at last. With my limbs still shaking from having escaped all this violence, I climb the gradient that leads to the dune.

There is still daylight, my body is dry now, and behind me the sea is calm and safe. The rest of the way seems predetermined, nearly finished, a victory in fact, but so fragile, provisional and uncertain that one could look in vain for any sign of it, and I feel no joy that will allow me to rest from my labours.

The sky is cloudy, uniform and low; the sandy moor is entirely grey in the early-morning light. I open the window to dispel the fog of half-sleep, but only a little air comes into the room. Outside, as usual, it is neither hot nor cold.

Perhaps this journey is not finished, perhaps this strand that I have just reached is only one more stop in an itinerary that will not yet come to an end; it has no white finishing post, so once again I shall have to pass through the turbulence and the froth. I still have many more tons of sand to disturb, and if the day is shining with such a pale glimmer, it is because it only has few hours of existence among the shadows... Or else, it would perhaps have been better to let myself sink under the waves and be carried away like a drowned man, away from this room which is gradually robbing me of my strength, my will, my life, far from these empty spaces where emaciated shrubs slowly stagnate under a sky that the sun does not manage to pierce with even the smallest sunbeam.

And so I shall finally have discovered the earth... the hard earth... perhaps... a stretch of fine sand, broken by rocks...

The hero turned over. Maurice... Moritz... Boris... He turned over in his bed to look once again at the big round alarm clock on the bedside table: its hands had hardly moved, it was not yet even eight thirty. And, with regret, Boris remembered that he had gone to bed early the night before, and therefore it was useless to try to go back to sleep. It would however have suited him very well, as the factory was not there to absorb the day, minute by minute, and to fill this great vacuum until tomorrow with thirty or forty hours of sleep; but it was better not to think about it, so limited were the possibilities in the circumstances: eleven or twelve hours, one could not expect more. And then, it would not have been altogether a solution.

The neighbour's radio was speaking, evenly and monotonously as if the announcer was reading a book that had no interest for him or for anyone else, and was not even certain that anyone was listening. On the floor above, a woman's voice was intermittently singing a tune that it was impossible to identify. The bells announced that Mass was about to begin. It was Sunday.

Lying on his back, the sheets half thrown back towards his feet, Boris began to study, above all to try to locate, in order to get rid of it more easily, the disagreeable sensation that was overcoming him, as it did every morning, starting in his head and travelling down through his body until it reached his hands and feet; the sensation quickly became unbearable and usually forced him to get out of bed. It was an impression of something absolutely smooth and flat that he could have chewed like a piece of rubber, but without managing to change its shape or spoil its perfect evenness, even though he tried to do so by gritting his teeth and forcing it to take the impression of his bite, to stick to the very surface of his teeth; one could even say that his teeth, by contamination, had themselves become quite flat, no longer capable of making an impression on anything, all the more so on this inert matter, on which any kind of grip could only be illusory.

Then suddenly, just as he had succeeded in grasping it with his front molars, the smooth surface of the lake suddenly became muddled, only to transform itself into a line of stylized little waves with identical curves repeating themselves at fixed intervals, moving from right to left with a uniform movement, slowly enough, with nothing unexpected to break the monotony.

Boris was not surprised at this sudden change, to which he was accustomed by now. He remained still for a long moment, making no motion, attentive, contemplating the situation. But he had to do something: the sharp point of successive craters, immobile in form, which pursued their exasperating course, seemed just then to conceal a threat as if some imminent rupture, a sudden disorder of design, was about to unleash a cataclysm upon him. But the course of events was not unknown: Boris methodically passed his tongue several times along the front of his top incisors until the little waves had completely left his mouth. But without his noticing it, they had taken refuge at the back of his cranium instead, just above his neck, a difficult place to access, and from which it would be even more difficult to dislodge them. By the time he had realized it, it was already too late. Only a natural intervention, such as a yawn, could end it, or else a sneeze or something similar.

As it was difficult waiting for that to happen by staying still, Boris reluctantly got up: it was barely nine o'clock in the morning.

The room came down to its measurable dimensions: a five-by-four-metre rectangle. The window, whose curtains he now opened wide, was in the middle of one of its short walls. The wooden rings slapped against each other as they were united to the left of the rail; the material folded back on itself against the night table where the large nickelled alarm clock stood. In the corner of the room, between the night table and the wall, was the divan. Boris pushed the sheets and blankets back towards the pillow and put the bedcover, with its faded motifs, back in its place on top.

As on every Sunday, he let his eyes fall for a few seconds on the little oil painting that was hanging on the wall between the foot of the bed and the door, seeing it again without either much pleasure or any particular dislike. It was a modest witness and all that he had been able to keep from the many canvases that he had produced in three or four feverish months several years earlier. Then he turned around and went over to the washbasin on the right side of the window. With very slow movements, he began to shave.

He chose a blade from among those already used during the preceding days and inserted it into the safety razor, screwing it as tightly as it would go and then unscrewing it a quarter-turn. He poured a little water from the jug into the basin, took the shaving brush from the shelf and started to lather his cheeks while looking at himself in the mirror. Pushing his face a little forward, he examined his skin carefully: on the whole it seemed to be in good condition, devoid of those slight irritations that sometimes made the job a delicate one. Only at the corner of his mouth had a few bristles grown, as usual parallel to the surface under a thin transparent film, but without having succeeded in penetrating through the outer skin. He opened his lips in order to stretch the skin and the uncooperative area next to it. His grimace widened, revealing his teeth. His lips curled back even more while his jaws clenched. This time the outside surface of his teeth was entirely visible throughout the whole length of the row. The index finger of his free hand passed slowly over his upper gums and over the tops of his teeth from the premolars of the one side to the premolars of the other, first in one direction, then in the other, five or six times.

His lips closed again; the brush was once more immersed in the basin and again it stroked his cheeks from top to bottom. Then his free hand moved the tip of the shaving soap over his jaws and chin and the brush began to rub again, but faster now. Having caught sight of the painting in the mirror, Boris turned round, his face half-soaped, to look at it again. It was red and purplish-brown, with here and there a few touches of mauve, grey and dark blue. A big mass of red first catches the eye, squarish and tinted with different nuances ranging from coral to brownish with a kind of vertical incision in the middle and uneven, almost black patches around it; on the far side of the canvas were elongated forms, columns or needles, repeated in the shadows, becoming more brightly coloured as they approached the centre and crossed the red object with its three uneven blue points. It portrayed nothing at all. The rectangle had been hanging up the other way round for a long time.

While completing his dressing without haste, Boris asked himself once more what he was going to do on this day off, one more day of which in any case he would retain no memory the following day. He was to meet Laura towards the end of the morning, but the prospect of having a discussion with her filled him with uneasiness in advance. Laura would ask him what he was doing at the moment; he would reply that he was doing nothing, that he was going to the factory, or else he would invent something or other, but she would not be taken in. The young woman would then try to make him "see sense", and he would not understand much of her argument. Without realizing it she would return to her own interests, the workers' movement, the more or less underground struggle, the progress of the organization. He would listen to her, as usual, with an astonishment mingled with a touch of boredom. And it would go on that way. He would hear stories he already knew, others of which he struggled to grasp the novelty or intricacies. After a while he would realize that he was not listening at all, that his mind was somewhere else, or nowhere at all. He would not even know for how long.

Sometimes Laura would stop of her own accord. He would then end up noticing it too. He would look at her a little uncomfortably and meet her wide-open eyes that looked at him as if he were some kind of strange animal, a monster, or even a void. She would ask him if he was not well; he would reply that no, it was just that he had a few problems, just like everyone else.

Boris sat down on the terrace, put the newspapers down on the table without opening them, ordered coffee and croissants and waited, his mind empty, letting his eyes wander at random over the crowd without seeing anything to catch his attention to even the slightest degree. People looked tired, which was all you could say about them. They walked by, indistinct and without expression. The scenery, which nothing was holding back any more, little by little slipped towards an area of mists, where the flat sea lapped the bottom of the rocks under a grey light.

The water is now completely calm. Not deep at this spot, but not transparent. It has a polished surface as if lacquered, from which large polished stones emerge, blackened and slippery, stripped of all seaweed. The unbending light leaves them no outline, while their contours are doubled by the reverse image of their reflections, neither more nor less precisely alike, but perhaps slightly more luminous so that they could easily be taken for the originals.

Farther away, the tidal line of rocks stretch out and multiply in low-lying chains, which gradually descend still as they move out along the coast to become no more than thin painted lines at their extremities. Still farther away the picture becomes blurred. But if I were to go farther down this side, I would only find the same rocks on the same immobile sea.

I live on an island, too far away from any continent to be able to think of getting away. Large ships sometimes pass in the distance, but do not change their course because of a few houses of little importance: we have nothing but moors, stones and sand. Fishermen and shepherds since the most ancient times, we live here in great isolation, not even able to hope, either for ourselves or our children, for any change from our miserable condition. Nevertheless, some people aspire to a different life, which is moreover impossible for them even to imagine, as they know of no pleasure other than the smell of grilling fish, and of no horizon other than that of the ocean.

Our village consists of nearly a score of thatched cottages, built of bluish slate, low and almost all grouped together on a piece of land that juts out at the extremity of a little bay that serves as a harbour for our boats. Behind it the land rises rapidly, leaving hardly any space for the narrow, sloping fields where we harvest our meagre crops of potatoes and rye; behind are the cliffs, where the sheep nourish themselves as best they can from the sparse short grass of which they are completing the destruction.

At the far end of the bay, and also on the other side across from the village, there are only swamps, several kilometres deep, broken up into brackish lagoons, and then beyond are the dunes, and once again the moor, more or less abruptly over the sea, joining imperceptibly, here and there, the sandy beaches or else the stone ridges where the kelp grows. The moors again stretch out over the interior, broken up here and there by muddy ground and peat bogs.

A low sky, hardly ever free of clouds, maintains a heavy humid presence over the landscape, hot but cottony and limiting the view to a few acres of greyness. But then we do not know the great cold that comes to other climes, where, it is said, life stops during the long winter months; our island never sees either the ice or the snow that we read about in books; the seasons here are so little differentiated that we often forget they exist. In the same way, during the frequent periods of fog, the night can hardly be differentiated from the day through the little windows of the smoky rooms where oil lamps burn without interruption.

The clouds that surround entwine their wisps among the gorse on the hillside, and stay there for whole weeks, forming and re-forming their shapes, allowing for an occasional glimpse of the wooden sails of a windmill or a few shelters for sheep. Anyone who is not a native of the locality can then easily lose their way in the labyrinth of paths that cross the moor, but as we all belong to the area no one risks getting lost; given that we have all had the leisure to come to know it by heart. As for strangers, we obviously never see any. Who, after all, even if such a thing were possible, would want to come here, where there is nothing to be earned and nothing to see?

The waiter, taciturn and silent, put the coffee on the table. Boris started on his breakfast, staring at a newspaper head-line without reading it, although the paper's date finally registered in his mind: Sunday the eighteenth of August. It was the eighteenth of August. He waited a good while in an attempt to get beyond this stage, then all at once the image returned: the regiments marching on the boulevards, the uniforms shining in the sunlight, the crowd picking up the military tunes while the beribboned instruments of the brass band swirled in unison above their heads... the nerv-ous prancing of the horses, the odour of manure, the shine of the drawn sabres... It was all a long time ago.

It was only by chance that a brief glance at the date had brought back their memory. The crowd that flowed past the terrace was the same as on any other Sunday and was no more thinking of parades than it was of fireworks. Men and women were going about their Sunday occupations at the same automatic pace as they went about their daily work, only a little better dressed, and all so much alike, so useless, their legs drooping and their arms swinging, without any purpose and for no reason.

And Boris, what was he waiting for, sitting in front of his cup? In one sense he was waiting for Laura, who had arranged to meet him there. But either Laura would come or she would not come, which in any case would not change anything as far as he was concerned. Nevertheless he looked at his watch. He simply wondered whether she would come.

The climate here is one you quickly get tired of: the swamps and the dunes themselves would take on different colours if the sun could only show itself for a few days. If the sun shone, then many flowers that now get nipped in the bud before they are even half open would bloom, instead of the withered corollas, green and rusty, with which we have to content ourselves when we stumble across them.

I dreamt of something red, as large as my hand, which was looking at me… If one day a tornado were to blow away the fog which stifles us, we would see the light rise in the sky, the sand would become hot, the sea green with golden reflections in the hollows of the waves, the moor would smell of honey... But we have always only known the sea and the mist, the light fine rain that falls for weeks without a whisper of wind to blow it away, slowly soaking through into the paths which give way underfoot with a squelching sigh, penetrating everywhere into the lofts and bedrooms, infiltrating people's clothes and even, over time, the grey matted wool of the sheep. The potatoes rot in the earth and the rye in the ear, the dried fish go black in the storerooms and the sheep's cheese in the cellars; everything we eat leaves a sour or mouldy aftertaste in the mouth.

Certainly we do not expect that the weather could become brighter for good. What cyclone or untoward event could suddenly come to trouble this immutable state of things, even for a day? It is difficult to image how such a suffocation could ever end: it would require, at the very least, changing the geographical location of the island. A more likely solution is that some boat, diverted from its course by some minor damage, would one day come to seek refuge in this little-known land, hoping to find a harbour, and then departing again as best it could, in the face of the poverty of the island, taking with it those who had come on board.

Would we then leave? Would we leave for ever these horizons where life, however monotonous, is still possible, in order to risk a different life under other skies, perhaps not able to endure the great cold or too much heat? Perhaps the thousand-year tolerance we have developed for living in this particular climate has marked our bodies to the point where we can no longer live anywhere else. The grey grasses of the moor would probably die if they were transplanted to another clime.

Boris looked at his watch again: it was useless to wait any longer. He put the newspapers that he had not yet unfolded back in his pocket, called the waiter, paid his bill and left. Laura would not be coming this morning.

2

OUTSIDE ON THE AVENUE this morning, the crowd, increasingly dense the more numerous it became, no longer seemed to be moving in one direction more than another. One could hardly talk of traffic, but rather of a loose agitation without any particular orientation, leaving behind zones of stagnation between which a few hurrying currents flowed intermittently, only to get lost again in the crowd.

Boris moved ahead with difficulty, cleaving a path between the bodies, taking advantage as best he could from the forward surges between the blockages. The effort he had to make to move ahead brought him back to his customary thoughts and, as usual, he was forced to realize that he too was going nowhere. At the same time he felt a viscous flow rapidly spreading through his whole body, entering his nose and ears with a muffled buzzing, filling his lungs with cachectic limbs and green faces.

Breathing with difficulty, he tried to cry out, but to call whom? And then again his head seemed to be filled with a grey soup as heavy as lead. He was only aware that the earth's surface was an immense bank of ice overseen by an enormous, solitary, frozen eye...

I am leaning over a pool, transparent but with the black and venomous appearance of dead waters; its bottom, which is very near, is indistinct and covered with a semi-decomposed slime which holds no insects on it; no green plant, sedge or ranunculus grows from its sides; its surface is not even spotted with duckweed. There are only a few little silver bubbles that emerge here and there from the brown foam; they rise gently into the open air and disperse without a sound, a bubble right near me, another a little farther away, then three or four in a row, another one on my side... one bubble... two bubbles... one bubble... Bubbles, little bubbles, rising slowly.

But the calm did not last long in this absolute tranquillity. Little melting flakes were at each instant appearing all over, a blink of the eyelids and brief movements of the pupil witnessed the derisory remains of life. A star, lit up for a moment, drew the eye from the depths of the shadows, where there was a spark, and a kind of promise that the fire would flare up again. And it was, in spite of everything, an event, so brief, sadly, that it could never quite come to life, an embryo set free too early, fallen for ever into the inert morass.

It was utopian now to believe that there were still some who pursued an uncomfortable path, built stone by stone in the midst of the ruins. If, moreover, a man, a solitary man, managed to follow the line of fire across the quicksands, where the ground gives way at each step, he would, day after day, be able to save his life, and at the same time he would pull along behind him a long procession of other men. Because it is only a will o' the wisp that dances over the peat bog, peopled with metaphors and mirages... Unless a few have been able to reach firm ground, after following, each in his own way, incommunicable paths.

A stronger current drew Boris towards a newspaper kiosk in front of which a human barrier had solidified. Although he could see neither the headlines nor the photographs between the heads, he stayed quietly where he was until the moment when a break in the crowd enabled him to force himself closer to the pages on display, which he then began to read mechanically.

Pressed against him, his fellow citizens, although more numerous than those one generally encountered around the news-stands, all seemed to be finding themselves there by chance, totally indifferent to the content of the articles

ALAIN ROBBE-GRILLET

they were reading. "Brilliant victory for the Church Party."
It might as well have been happening in the antipodes.

"Brilliant victory…" A stone shot across the sky like a
meteor and disappeared, breaking, in its fall, the tranquil
surface of a deep green waterhole between the flat rocks.
Boris now found himself far away from the kiosk, in the
middle of a thinner crowd where it was once again possible to walk; he made an effort to escape the attraction of
the green water, which was gradually disappearing under
his steps at the same time as the phrases of the newspaper
formed themselves again in front of his eyes, accompanied
this time by all their meaning: "Brilliant victory for the
Church Party. Its success has surpassed all our expectations:
we have won nearly 50% of the seats in the large cities, and
40% in the country as a whole."

Boris took from his pocket the morning edition of *Action*,
which had already announced in large letters the results of
the general election. The provisional figures announced
there were more or less the same: 38% of the votes were
going to the Church Party, about 30% to the Unionists,
a few less to the Democrats, the other 5% being divided
between the Royalist Party and two or three groups of even
lesser importance; but, as in previous years, when it was

22

all added up, it did not amount to more than one tenth of those entitled to vote.

The last poll only confirmed the one fact: quite simply, the country had almost totally abstained from showing up at the polling stations. Without going so far as to make, through this collective defection, the kind of gesture that would have been achieved by, for example, the placing of several million unmarked ballot papers in the boxes, or the organization of marches and political rallies during the election campaign, the great majority of the population had let it be understood in this way that it was totally disinterested in the affairs of state. While passively observing the laws, which seemed to them to be sufficiently reasonable not to provoke too much violent reaction, the citizens, for the most part, had long lived in almost complete ignorance of the disagreements within the government, or of the agreements momentarily reached between the King, the parliament and the different parties.

Boris tried to remember a less stagnant period that he might have known earlier, a period when public events still interested the masses: ten or twelve years ago, parliament had been dissolved after a series of popular uprisings; there had been clashes between demonstrators and police, many hurt and some probably dead. With hindsight, though, it seemed that there could hardly have been much connection between the blood that had been spilt on the pavements and the innocuous stories of corruption that had occurred earlier, cleverly orchestrated, it is true, by an effective press campaign. It was summer, it was hot, the day had ended with arguments in the beer halls: "It's a scandal, sir! Thousands of honest people reduced to misery!" This was not altogether true. Everyone, afterwards, had gone home.

There had also been the attempt on the life of the Prince Regent, but that event had been kept much more in the dark, even for those who had honestly tried to find out what had happened; and there had been few of those because in those faroff days, even then… in those faroff days… even then…

The narrow ribbon of sand left by the high tide along the length of the dunes is broken again by a rocky promontory which goes down into the sea. With the facility that comes from long habit, I climb the piled-up rocks, following a path known since childhood.

The water at this hour of the day flows deeply into a labyrinth of semi-submerged tunnels and gorges with a continual gurgle of coming and going. Heart beating fast, striding across legendary chasms, I avoid the customary passages leading to those advanced positions where the flat sea laps softly against the rounded rocks whose conquest it has left until later. Between the last blocks that it lets emerge, a kind of natural basin comes into being, green and deep, only communicating with the open sea by means of a narrow channel; on the surface, at least, because the water is lit from below by all the light of a great liquid mass. And I remain fascinated by the intense glow that comes from this other world, where, very gently, as expected, I let myself sink in...

Boris became aware, because of the cold that was suddenly overtaking him, that he was no longer standing upright on the solid rock, but was now in the middle of an abyss that was rapidly swallowing him. He clenched his fists in his pockets as hard as he could, even digging his nails into his palms; indistinct shapes were moving around him, the row of houses on his right oscillated once, twice, then recovered its equilibrium. Someone was still holding him up, but he disengaged himself politely. "It's nothing, I'm going home." The green water had disappeared again, and he continued to walk along the boulevard.

He should not let himself get caught up like this, just because that, for now, was the choice he had made.

The suffrage, that the ancient constitution persisted in calling universal, meant no more, when all was said and done, than the votes of a few fanatics like Laura, which were swamped by the ballots that the different parties bought from the poorest classes. And as, contrary to what some believed, the custom of selling one's vote did not seem to extend to more than a few million individuals, the big parliamentary groups each represented only three or four per cent of the total number of electors listed on the registers.

In spite of this, the country's situation was alarming: the administration was incompetent, manufacturing was chaotic, finances were desperate; as for foreign relations, they were in such an imprudent mess that in the general opinion a catastrophe would occur from one day to the next, and no one dared affirm that the country could come out of it unscathed. Everyone felt that their possessions, their very existence even, were tied up in this business, but even though there was only a tiny minority that went on saying that the problem had no reasonable solution, people thought it fairly unlikely that one did exist that had not already been discovered by the many generations of specialists who had been seriously looking for it.

Those who voted, whether by conviction or because they were short of money, often affected to think of the others as traitors, or at least as cowards; this judgement was only valid from the point of view of a party that would eventually attract their support. Indeed, none of the heads of the parties failed to suggest implicitly in their speeches that all the abstainers belonged "in their hearts" to their particular group, so each one of them spoke in the House in the name of the entire nation, and that without risking the slightest contradiction from the others.

Without straining logic any further, the Church Party was at present glorying in a small gain of a few hundred thousand votes, which, however large this might seem in relation to the total number of voters for this party or even to the total number of all the voters, only constituted a handful in comparison with the tens of millions of hearts which were supposed to be beating for the Church.

Certainly, Boris was not taken in by these propaganda devices, which were only good enough to deceive children. Nothing had really changed; even if a new majority were to establish itself in parliament, even if the King had to reshuffle his ministers, the ninety million phantom voters would continue to represent the real country and, ultimately, they were the ones who counted. And, in this sense, it was certain in any case that those in power represented the general opinion, because it was easier for them to upset any particular interest group with impunity than to take any initiative that would awaken the masses that supported none of them. That was why the important changes in law which figured in the party electoral programmes were never seriously proposed by their mandated defenders, so dangerous did it seem to them to get the assembly to adopt a reform, the promise of which had not attracted the country to the ballot boxes. Any group that took advantage of its fleeting majority to try to force through such a measure would in fact be taking the risk, apart from the remote possibility of a popular rising, of seeing a few malcontents who were in disagreement breaking out of their silence the following year and throwing their weight on the other side, thereby upsetting the clever combinations of bought electorates.

In general, the politicians considered that ideas were dangerous, and only made use of them in rare and confused speeches that the newspapers relegated to the back pages. There was therefore no question of putting them into practice in the management of the state, so that, in a sense, the doctrines expounded could remain even more perfect by not coming out of their abstract state. Only a handful of the most showy ones served from time to time as smokescreens in certain particularly dubious schemes; but on reflection they quickly became as difficult to understand as the rest of the theories. When talking of monetary systems, the economy, education, taxes, they were really referring to something different. Different conceptions of order, liberty, justice; the essence was always somewhere else.

Justice, however… justice! The word passed whistling through the cylinders of a wheezy machine, actively compressed, and was then blown out in long bursts of vapour – juss tiss juss tiss juss tiss – in order to fall at the end onto the ground, colourless, disarticulated, bereft of significance… Around its remains, the earth took on a greenish tint, that of deep water surrounded by rocks… Boris looked away.

He tried once again to reconstitute a coherent summary of the doctrines, but the urgency of the danger succeeded in making this task impossible. One after the other, the words turned round in his head with the accelerated rhythm of a steam turbine; the latter seemed to be on the point of racing away when it suddenly stopped just in front of the words "Major Construction Works", which began to float gently in the air and then came and settled on a red sign – "Caution! Major Construction Works" – blocking off a view of fences and building sites, abandoned it seemed; although it was Sunday, there was nothing extraordinary about that. There at least the images were solid and comforting.

Left and right, between corrugated iron huts, irregular scaffolding – a tangle of iron girders and wooden planks – rose into the air. Platforms had been erected to carry little hand winches and electric cranes; most of the equipment looked as if it had already seen much service. And, looking a little closer, one could see that the work had been interrupted quite some time ago, perhaps indefinitely: the enclosure, crumbling in many places, revealed piles of rubbish which was disappearing under the weeds and half-dug wells overflowing with empty tins and every kind of rubbish. The earthworks, which had barely been started, were already being used as a refuse dump. He even ought to hurry to get away from all this waste.

The parties, although they had been in agreement on the necessity of carrying out these building works, had disagreed fundamentally as to their nature: some wanted to establish a network of new roads, others wanted to replace agricultural equipment or to build cathedrals. The public only played a

small part in these debates, not even showing much enthusiasm for the government's project, which began with the
erection of huge retirement homes. During the years that
the discussions had been going on, no agreement was ever
reached, so that nothing was ever started; and each party
remained convinced of the superiority of their own course
of action.

For some time Boris had been dreaming confusedly of
neat piles of bricks and of noisy workshops; then, exhausted
by the effort, he walked on with an even step, thinking of
nothing at all.

On a rocky shore a waterhole, narrow and deep, whose
level rises and falls, calmly, regularly, according to the
movements of the sea. The sandy bottom gives the clear
water a luminous, green transparency. The high tide must
be steady.

Purple reflections on the sides indicate tufts of seaweed
growing along the rocks; perhaps it is growing three or four
metres down. On the surface a line of white froth, very thin,
imperceptibly drifts towards the channel.

All of a sudden something falls with a "plop" and a splash
of spray; the concentric waves reflected on the periphery

burst out through the water, soon absorbed by the calming motion of the waves.

Now one can see no more than a hole of placid water which sways slightly as it laps against the stones.

Boris looked at the newspaper which he was still holding in his hand without realizing it. "Brilliant victory..." The page, rolled into a ball, was dropped into the green water; a slight breeze carried it out to sea.

My eyes follow this ball of paper for a long time as it drifts away.

After it disappears from sight, I continue on my way, along the seashore beyond the rocky spur. The sea starts to go out again. The terns, tossing their heads, stride along the line of algae they have just abandoned. The birds flee before me, always keeping the same distance, sometimes swallowing some tiny crustacean with a rapid movement of the beak.

Their feet leave precise, tortuous designs behind them, little crooked crosses which disappear by themselves in the wet sand.

3

THE MONDAY MORNING PAPERS did hardly more than repeat the news of the day before in various forms: *Action* sang out the triumph of the Church Party and let it be clearly known that a new era had begun, while each of the other parties tried to convince its respective supporters that its lack of success was only an illusion behind which one could divine a real reaffirmation of their strength.

The larger-circulation newspapers only gave a few statistics and very brief commentaries, the large headlines being reserved for the mysterious death – murder or suicide – of a foreign student whose body had just been discovered by accident after several days of futile search. Every newspaper showed the same photograph, dating from some years earlier, showing the young man playing with a large black dog.

Boris glanced through all the columns, including those devoted to sport, put the pages back in order and folded them carefully.

He was nearly there; the tramway ran by a series of tall houses with narrow windows of which the flat façades could only be distinguished from each other by the differences in their green covering or by the colour they were painted. Just beyond the turning the great gate of the General Factory appeared in the middle of the patchwork rubble wall of the enclosure, in front of which, about fifty metres farther on, was the stop.

Boris climbed down in the middle of a group of workers whom he did not know, went through the gate with them, showing his pass, and started to move towards Workshop Z.

In the entrance hall the familiar odour of hot oil and steel dust immediately greeted him. His timecard had been displaced on the board; he took a few seconds to find it, then put it through the clock, then, rapidly, he climbed the little staircase that led to his office.

Making his way through the gallery which overlooked the machines from above, he could see the eight rows of lathes and milling machines and the workers bending over them, their faces already spotted with grease. The glass partition barely reduced the sound of the motors and the grinding of machine tools, but helped to create an impression of unreality or of infinite distance, giving the impression of a reversed telescope.

Once the office door was closed, the noise was no more than an incessant humming whose very continuity helped one to forget it.

Boris took off his overcoat, sat at his desk and started to contemplate the pieces of paper filled with figures that covered it; he still had several days to go before he would complete the series of calculations, after which the next series would follow on: it never varied much. Thomas, his colleague, had not yet arrived.

From the window he could see the grey uninterrupted wall of the building which occupied the other side of the alleyway; it was called Unit Eight, and it must be very sombre inside. The concrete was very old and of a very shabby appearance: it was cracked from top to bottom, and large plaques had fallen off it and in many places pieces had been pulled away, leaving an aspect of lighter-coloured, more crumbly-looking mortar, half-decomposed by the rain which had created irregular swellings disintegrated by the wind. On the jagged edges of the craters, the sand has gathered in moving furrows and is rubbing against the hard grasses.

Walking is slow and difficult in this crumbling terrain; one ripple follows another, filled with the same rigid blue plants from which at every step one can detach in their dozens the little striped snails, as dry as the nettles they eat.

The sea, from which I have been distancing myself little by little, is now only present to the ear; the view all around is now limited to the tops of the dunes...

The door opens, the horizon of soft lines is broken. The boss put his head around it, in a hurry as usual:

'Thomas is not coming in today. See if he had anything urgent to do. He'll be away a few days. The crash was quite serious!"

The last word fell, hitting the desk and the floor with a clear tinkle of stones on a ground hardened by frost.

Boris did not respond right away, and the metallic vibration decreased quickly; when it had been completely drowned by the background hum of the machines, it was already too late. The air regained its colloidal consistency, like a translucid puddle that had spread out in all the directions in which an explosion had distributed it. The boss swiftly retired and, to reduce the damage he had caused, closed the door behind him.

Inside the room, Boris tried to get up, to at least move his leg, but without succeeding; he therefore remained immobile.

The atmosphere became syrupy; it even coagulated here and there in big pale clots which slowly passed by, filling up the room and gluing itself to the walls, slowing down his embolism in this way.

The clock, which hung above the big wooden filing cabinet, counted off the minutes in an ever more dubious fashion, dissociating them from each other; having arrived at the bottom of the dial, the minute hand stopped altogether, being incapable of following an itinerary so devoid of sense. A very obscure silence, in the midst of which thought itself seemed to have lost its meaning, established itself between the ceiling, the window and the door. Eternity was all-consuming.

In the middle of this frozen silence, the telephone, which had remained untouched, now began to ring; as Boris stretched out his arm towards it, the minute hand once again began to climb with its usual regularity.

A faroff voice asked for Thomas. Boris answered that he was not in the office and hung up. Insensibly, like the slow accumulation of silt deposits, the valleys of sand took shape again.

A twisting path revealed purple patches of nettles on the left, while ahead of me a shallow depression could be seen, covered with a low, dry vegetation, and in the background it the path, which feet had traced out. On the land side on the right, there was a progressive rise and the indistinct line of the dunes disappearing into the fog.

We are in the middle of winter, the schools of seasonal fish have left our shores, our meagre harvest has long since been stored in the granaries, the necessary reparations to the houses have been finished for this year. It is the season when, less than ever, nothing is urgent.

The sheep, nearly all dried off, do not need much attention in spite of the little food they can find to eat in the enclosures where the grass is now half rotten. Yesterday I had to augment their rations with a few sheaves of badly dried straw taken from the reserves.

I went out early this morning to open the door of the sheep pen to give them more time to find their own subsistence. In the woolly half-light, the flock hurried off towards the cliff, quickly absorbed into the fog where the sound of their braying was swallowed up, the same fog that has seldom left us for the last two months.

We are in the middle of winter, and yet the aspect of the country has scarcely changed: often in midsummer we have long periods of mist, but at present it is the greater than usual idleness which makes the horizon seem heavier and more indistinct, the sea a little more flat and the plain a little more grey.

After looking after the sheep this morning and drinking a bowl of milk which I had just drawn from the udder, I followed the road along the big enclosures which run alongside the cliffs, nibbling the chunk of bread that I had brought with me; the air was so humid that the crust very quickly became soft with a disagreeable taste of damp, so much so that I put the rest in my pocket in order to toast it later. I went on my way through the peat bog, thinking of nothing.

Shining droplets were suspended on the spiders' webs between the branches of the heather. Sometimes a whole web, full of water, barred the way and was clinging to my legs, deeply drenching the all too light material of the garment.

I walked faster to get warm, and as far as the dunes on the west, among which I wandered haphazardly. One undulation succeeds another, each one alike and covered with the same blue vegetation encrusted with little snails. Difficult as it is to make progress in this crumbling terrain, I feel no tiredness; but I have the impression all the same that for some hours I have been turning in circles in the sand and the mist...

Suddenly, by the chance of a fleeting sunny spell, I think I see the back of a man a few metres ahead of me, but a moment later the curtain of cloud descends again and I find myself alone, doubting that I have really seen anything at all.

Indeed, it would be quite astonishing for another person to be walking along this coast, where I never meet anyone.

But then, once again, I see for a moment this large, slightly bent back which seems to be showing me the way. Without a thought of the return route, I penetrate ever farther ahead into this deserted area, abandoned even by the nettles. Why should I have to return to the village? We are in the middle of winter, a period where there is no pressing work and nothing is waiting for me anywhere.

Little by little the landscape around me is changing: the ground is flatter, the grass has become more sparse; at the same time the sky has cleared slightly to let the view extend to the flat shore of a largely open bay...

And I can still see this man whom I do not know, who is also walking alongside the sea.

In the canteen, the discussion had become far-ranging since the beginning of lunch. Arnand had raised, with renewed zeal, the subject of politics and, contrary to their usual custom, the others had responded.

At the beginning some of them had said that politics didn't interest them, but they were rightly given the riposte that the subject certainly concerned them, which they took to be a crafty attack on the principle of their independence, so much so that they ended up listening to his exposition of the situation with bad grace.

For Arnaud the matter was simple: experience had shown that no coalition of parties could last long, as a result of their conflicting demands, and the relative majority that the Church had won in parliament now allowed it really to take control of the country and consequently apply to it, gradually of course, its ambitious plan for reform. In the meantime we were about to see begin – from tomorrow it was said – the great building programme that no one until now had been able to set in motion; in the face of the success that had been achieved, the masses would not take long to recognize the excellence of these principles and they would collaborate in good faith in a communal enterprise. In the ranks of the other parties there were certainly some honest men to be found who would rally to the right cause without hesitation; as for the others, they would be prevented from doing any harm.

Protestations were made all round the table: on the one hand the Church Party had already had the opportunity of exercising power and had not done so; on the other hand it was by no means certain that the new orientation of public affairs would lead to any tangible results any time soon, and certainly such results would not please everyone. And then, even admitting all that, must we conclude that all these measures will be enough to attract their sincere loyalty to the system as a whole? As for the idea of not letting the opposition put their point of view, it was judged to be unacceptable, and it was said that Arnaud – or the Church Party – was going a bit too far. From all sides it was shouted out that this was dictatorship.

To add to the confusion, some jokers brought quite outrageous arguments into the discussion, of which many were then discussed, while at the same time serious propositions were taken to be wisecracks. And as a result, everyone forgot to make the usual criticisms of the poor quality of the food.

It was then, in the general tumult, that this phrase was distinctly heard: "What is needed is to kill the King!"

Immediately a shocked silence fell on the table. The suggestion was in any case very strange, the King himself being, if not particularly popular, generally considered to have no real importance and to be perfectly harmless. Everyone asked himself with perplexity who it was who had advanced this remedy, because in the general disorder no one knew where the voice had come from. The idea seemed to be stupid, because it would neither serve the interests of the Church, nor of its adversaries, nor of anyone else, but if it was only a facetious remark, its author did not disclose himself in order to receive the credit for it; unless he had taken fright after the fact at his own effrontery. But this last fear was not, on reflection, very likely, because there was no special taboo surrounding the sovereign, and on this subject as on all others, there was an absolute liberty of expression.

Arnaud, upset by not having understood what had just happened, no longer thought of continuing his arguments; he was afraid of being held responsible for an embarrassment which he had somehow originated, and perhaps even of being accused of being a murderer. Someone concluded, voicing the general opinion: "It's stupid to say things like that."

Boris briefly talked about the accident that had happened to Thomas: a lorry had knocked him down on Saturday morning and, although he had no serious injury that was apparent, he would have to stay in bed for a few days.

Everyone deplored this misfortune and went off to smoke one or two quiet cigarettes beside the chimneys and the blackened walls.

In his office, the massive silhouette was waiting for Boris.

The bay that we had been following ended in a tongue of land without any particular feature, hardly higher than the beach and only distinguished at its extremity by a rocky elevation, the last vestige of some very old building. It was here that the man had stopped, looking out to sea, apparently scrutinizing the movement of the waves.

I have not often come to these parts: there is no fishing in summer on this part of the coast and the soil produces nothing of value; it is uniform and hard, like fine gravel driven by the wind, or rather by the great tides which must penetrate quite far into this flat terrain, which is protected neither by rocks nor dunes. Salt deposits bear witness, leaving a contamination of white circles on the surface between the rare little sickly plants: some have little thick leaves, but a grey crust takes away any appearance of life, while others are reduced to a dry and hairy bud low on the ground, lichens on which the stains look like the marbling of diseased soil.

As I hang back to get a closer look, I notice, on raising my eyes, that the contemplator has left his promontory and is walking on.

Now he seems to be walking faster, soon he will disappear altogether into a hollow that cannot be seen from where I am. The sand is so compact and heaped up at this spot that one might think it is a crumbling rock disintegrating; the black strands of seaweed brought up by the sea crack underfoot.

The silhouette emerges far off on top of a crater and then disappears again. The sea coast, far off, resumes its irregular murmurs. I turn round in order to get back before nightfall. Who was it after all who had used that phrase and why?

4

A T THE SOUND OF A LITTLE TRUMPET, the three
vehicles, full to breaking point, rattled into motion.
Arriving at the turning, they were still moving so slowly
that five or six latecomers, running out through the big
gate, managed to jump onto the running boards, holding
on to the human clusters that were already hanging out
over the platforms. Bodies were being pushed about inside,
accompanied by murmurs of protestation from those being
squashed. Then the convoy picked up a little speed.

Boris found himself narrowly squeezed between two strangers who were talking across his face as if he did not exist;
Vincent, with whom he had walked out of the factory, had
been separated from him during the assault on the tramway.

"Did you see the man who was shot down?"

"Who? The student?"

"Red, he's called. A funny name."

Their opinions were divided: for the first speaker he was
a foreigner, therefore a spy whom the police had liqui-
dated, and they had been right to do so; the other one,

less loquacious and more colourful, opted for a crime of passion.

Boris tried to pull himself away from the conversation between the two men. Fortunately some people were getting off, which made this easier; the xenophobe took advantage of the free space around himself to unfold the evening paper.

A large picture decorated the front page; Boris immediately recognized the abandoned building site that he had wandered past during his walk the previous day: the same bizarre scaffolding bristling with disintegrating materials, the same falling-down shacks and the same piles of rubbish. A caption in bold type related how the body had been found in this vacant lot in the suburbs. Struck by this coincidence, Boris searched through his memories to clarify his own impression, but this, on the contrary, only had the effect of effacing it more and more, so much so that soon he was left with nothing but a slight uneasiness. And then he had never left the centre of town yesterday, which was not marred by any building site, ancient or modern; how had these images become connected in his mind? All of Sunday now evoked no more than big stone buildings, richly ornamented and standardized. He even began to doubt in the end that the shock he was feeling could really have been caused by some landscape that had somehow remained in his memory. But what else was there?

The tram had gradually emptied itself and a seat that had become free allowed him to sit down. After all, there had been nothing very remarkable in this confusion of metal and scaffolding, the remains of some construction work interrupted by the recession. The wild grass had grown here and there over the debris which littered the ground; usable pieces had been pulled away wherever it was possible – burnable wood, fragments of sheet metal that would fit over the roof of a cabin – while at the same time the space had been littered with unwanted domestic cast-offs. The only special feature to distinguish the place from those like it, which were very numerous on the outskirts, lay in its unusual dimensions, which gave away the considerable importance of the enterprise that had been undertaken, one of the grandiose projects of which all that now remained were the crumbling skeletons and the excavated holes half-filled in by the rubble.

Boris walked on, through a jumble of old buckets and stoves eaten away by rust, when he saw at his feet, on the path carved out by children's games, a flat stone, horizontal and barely higher than the earth. To all appearances it was a tombstone: one could clearly see the little cross followed by the laconic inscription, roughly and newly engraved, it seemed:

*Ci-gît Red**

At this moment a long and piercing whistle sounded in his ears and at the same time the three words moved about, only to reappear in an accusatory anagram:

Regicide!

The lights went on in the tram, although it was still light enough outside; Boris looked at his head in the brightly lit glass, through which a display of carrots and cabbages could be seen passing.

The room I am entering is sombre; under the low beams the tobacco smoke mixes in the thick air with the more acid odour of the peat; the daylight which filters through the tiny windows is only just enough for me to find my way to the table, where I can barely see the faces of those who

---

* "Here lies Red".

are sitting there. Nevertheless, I walk in without fear and I find an empty place on the bench: only my friends could be sitting there, the men of the village.

An earthenware goblet passes from hand to hand, filled with this bitter drink that we make from malted grain. Nothing is said. One can only hear the sound of sucking on a pipe and the cracking of a peat fire that is too damp, in the great chimney which pulls badly. Like the others, I smoke in silence.

Little by little my eyes get accustomed to the gloom; around me are gathered blind Alban, Malter the bonesetter, the two brothers Guilhem and Guiraut, Peire with his dog lying down sleeping next to him on the tile floor, old Venant, young Venant, Maur and Marc, my fishing companions, blond Eric, and over there Guérin the seventh, who, even sitting down, is a head taller than any of us. Farther away, the end of the long table is so badly lit that I cannot see who is sitting there.

The goblet goes around, and from time to time someone fills it up from the jug...

Guiraut says, weighing each word: "The body was the colour of a living flame." Then he draws on his pipe and falls back into his thoughts.

We are turned towards him, gravely signalling our agreement, but no one makes any comment. He must have told his story before my arrival; I therefore make no attempt to find out what it's about: I am too young, and he is not going to start all over again to tell something that must already have been very long in the telling to judge by the speed of his delivery. It must have been about some fabulous fish that he had caught earlier or that he had perhaps only just seen.

The minutes pass; everyone smokes in silence. It seems to be my turn to tell something.

"There was someone outside today, over by the dunes."

Nobody answers; the faces look round to deduce who could still be walking outside at this time. I realize that I have spoken out of turn, because what was I doing there myself? Nevertheless I go on, anxious to finish: "Someone I didn't know, walking along the shore."

That is all there is, I stop, the story is told. And yet it was rather like a distant horn sounding. What could I add that would make them understand what language cannot express? The others say nothing either.

Behind the blue-stained panes the night has arrived. It is completely black. Marc, the youngest, stands up and carefully puts more peat on the fire; nobody lights the lamp, out of respect for Alban. The smoke has now become so thick that it is difficult to breathe.

I am thinking that I will not get an explanation, but then the voice of Venant the elder raises itself in the shadows: "It must have been the man in the tower, Malus the hermit."

I go on: "I've never seen this man."

"That's because you're so young."

Once again there is the sound of beer being poured and the gurgling of a pipe bowl. Only the fire, which Marc has revived, lights up the room, making gigantic shadows dance along the length of the walls. Fast asleep, the old dog whines faintly in his dream.

"I've already seen the man you're talking about. Once I even caught his empty gaze, which most of the time is directed towards the surface of the sea, as if he were waiting for some message. His tower is over there towards the north, at the extremity of the point, among the wave-beaten rocks."

"Why doesn't he live with us? Why does he never come to the village?"

"I don't know."

In the black heart of night, Marc and I walk side by side. At the end of the street, where the paving stones end, we separate: each goes home to sleep. A gust of wind brings the smell of the low tide up from the bottom of the bay.

Mounting the stairs, Boris recognized Laura's footsteps climbing behind him. He opened the door just as she caught up. They went in.

Laura, who had spent the day in meetings and debates, seemed to be exhausted; she let herself drop into the armchair and looked at Boris without saying anything, seeking the right angle from which to attack.

He did not feel in good enough form to put up a serious resistance; uneasy without knowing why, he asked himself if it would not be better to tell her everything that had happened to him since the day before. It was a difficult task, because nothing in fact had happened to him, and the few impressions that he believed he had retained fled his mind the moment he tried to pin them down. The very little that Laura could get out of him would be of very little interest to her, yet she would not have made the effort to come just to listen to fairy tales. On the other hand it would have been important to bring up certain matters that were not too confused in his mind in order to see what they were all about; but where to start? There had been valleys and plains, rivers with flat banks that he never followed to the end, there had been flat waters smothered in water lilies; and what beside?

Boris opted for these words: "You didn't come yesterday", which was at least an objective statement and did not involve him in too much controversy.

Laura made an effort to come out of her torpor. She knew from experience that the atmosphere of this room was bad for her; she could divine the pitfalls and trapdoors that awaited her everywhere, ready to swallow up anyone who dozed off. Sitting opposite her, Boris breathed in the odours of the night.

Barely a hundred metres away, the returning tide was bringing the bay into existence. The regular sound of the surf guides the feet towards the seashore; the polished shingle leads on to the tiny gravel, then comes the soft sand, interspersed by ridges of little hard stones. Farther on the feet sink into hollow clay pits of which the faded stench is mingled with the perfume of iodine and salt. It is night. The sea is low. Come on, Laura. The wet sand is soft under our bare feet, the water is lukewarm on our legs; come and walk through the moving strands of vegetation, come and listen, Laura, to the night songs of the sirens...

After a few seconds, as if it had been hesitating, the flow of the rising tide gives, among the disturbed algae, the signal for the charge.

"No, I didn't come, I didn't have the time," the young girl started off.

"You never have the time," said Boris; but not in a tone of reproach.

"The elections gave us a lot to do," she went on. "It all went very well: you saw the results. Immediately afterwards we had to organize the demonstration for the National Day celebration; not many turned out, but it was a beginning."

"The papers never even mentioned a demonstration. What are you going to do now?"

The Church's plan was very simple. It consisted of making the population aware of the peril which menaced it and, without creating unnecessary panic, showing it that a disaster was imminent, but not inevitable. The awakening of public concern would be accompanied by massive propaganda in favour of the Church which "alone was capable of bringing the insurmountable problem of the hour to an end" and, at the same time, of keeping a firm hand on the government.

All this would happen as far as possible without any discord: no scandals in the Chamber, no brawls in the streets;

the incidents of Sunday night, which happened during the procession, had been carefully damped down, and could hardly damage the party of law and order; the general desire for calm, which had been appealed to by one side, could not be imperilled by the other. But at the same time, by a gradual mobilization of minds, each citizen would find himself more and more "ready to go into battle" and would become, without knowing it, "a soldier of the Church in the service of the community".

Boris immediately worried about the role the King would play in all this. The question seemed of lesser importance to Laura: the sovereign, naturally enough, would continue, as in the past, to be discreet and support the strongest faction. And now the supremacy of the Church was now legally confirmed by having obtained a majority of votes, and would only assert ever more strongly now that there would be more and more supporters flocking towards it. At the right moment a new election would validate the progress that had been made, killing off the rival factions and demonstrating that it was the real people who made the law after all. The undecided would then rush to support their victory.

To make things clearer, the Church would effectively break off its relations with the other parties, justifying this by pointing out their doctrinal differences, which were not in short supply. During ten years of frequent compromise, alliances had been made that gave evidence of less intransigence, but the professional dialecticians would find it easy to explain all that, in an effort to reconcile the differences, the failure of which would serve as one more reason for why it was necessary to bring matters to a head. It would remind everyone quite clearly from which party the ideas really originated, and that would, what's more, give some satisfaction to the theoreticians themselves; their ideas would be paraded out again on the occasion of their retirement, while at the same time appeasing the real militants who would be asking just where the "overwhelming need for action" was going.

Indeed, it was around their little kernel of good intentions that the system of the future would be built, and not on the buying of the voters' ballot papers, as had previously been the practice. It was recognised that the latter policy led to nothing positive: it had been honestly used in order to accomplish what was best for the citizens in spite of themselves; but faced with the impossibility of succeeding in this way, they would, on the contrary, appeal for the free vote of each citizen.

Even the most reticent among the leaders of the Church were forced to recognize the soundness of this method. As each party reserved all its financial resources to bribe the electors, the smallest increase in payment that was proposed, so much had the number of claimants increased, could only have the effect of diminishing the advantage to the beneficiaries of the vote; and a kind of rate of exchange had therefore been established for the price of a vote, which varied very little and established the equilibrium between the buying power of the parties and that of their supporters; and therefore the canvassers, in order to be convincing, had to use psychological arguments, such as flattery and promises, as if they were undertaking a real electoral campaign.

They were going to get rid of all this bureaucratic and policing organization, whose principle task had been to prospect in the poorer quarters for naive or badly informed sellers of their votes, who would give their ballot paper at a low price. What was really needed were people of good faith (like Boris) in order to build up an ever-growing and active circle. Therefore it was necessary for them to come out of their dreams and to help organize the state, instead of continuing to live in chaos. If such people had until now been thought of as a nuisance, that was not – she said – because of their sincerity, but because of their indecision.

Boris had listened as best he could; he sensed that the time had come for him to reply. The only important fact that had occurred to him was that the King was not included in any of these projects. He said, without really thinking about it: "It's becoming dark, in a few hours the sea will be in again."

Laura made a gesture of impatience; she had no time to lose on dreamers. In other circumstances she might have been interested by this declaration, but for her the sea had not stopped rising. She rapidly took her leave.

Once alone, Boris began to laugh irresistibly, without knowing why, an immense and silent laugh.

The clouds block the sky in violet bars, parallel to the horizon; nevertheless the air is dryer and lighter than usual, the faraway distance is lit with that slightly misleading clarity that one sees just before the rain.

I am walking towards the north. Flocks of crows fly around me, accompanying me on my way with their cries and the beating of their wings. The sky is black, the earth is black, it is about to rain.

At the very end of the island, on the outermost point, stands the old tower where the Hermit looks out at the ocean, night and day. That is where I am going; over the plain, by the side of the cliffs, along the sea coast, I am heading for the north: in the sand and through the bogs, as if I have been walking for ever, I go on implacably towards the north where the man in the tower is awaiting me.

It is time, it is time; I hear, from the top of the belfry, the bells that call me towards the north.

5

ON TUESDAY MORNING Boris woke up with a heavy and painful headache. He thought at first that a little cold water would clear away this nocturnal detritus, dirty and encumbering, that still remained in his head, his neck, even in his limbs; but he did nothing at all about it: a powerful migraine took over instead and far from disappearing over breakfast, it only grew with every movement he had to make to get ready and go to work.

Even though he was quite motionless, the pain took him over piteously: every sound he heard went through his head from one temple to the other and, once there, instead of leaving as it had entered, it rebounded, echoing to infinity through the columns and the vaults, looking for an exit. After the clanging symphony of rubbish bins and milk cans in the street, there came the grinding of the tramways in the middle of honking horns and, after all that, the workshop, where the horrible hammering finished him off.

Once in his office, he stood leaning against the closed door and put his hand over his eyes. No sound now came from the outside world, the room was quiet, everything was resting calmly where it belonged, but it only made it worse for all that to feel the infernal beating in his head of all the shocks he had stored up, which hammered on the walls of his skull from all directions. He had the feeling of being enclosed in a cellar with an army of workers all forging arms, and of impotently assisting in the preparation of a war which he wanted to stop.

He sat at his desk to attempt all the same to take up his calculations at the point where he had left them the previous evening, but the figures jumped around in front of him so that he could make no sense of them; it was with great difficulty that he succeeded in patiently coming up with a few figures, even though he was not sure of many of them, so that there could be no question of attempting to do anything serious with them, even on a machine.

Boris put down his papers and let his eye wander outside the window. The wall of Unit Eight was even more off-putting than usual.

Vincent, who had come to fetch him for lunch, found him among the scattered pieces of paper, looking into space with a dazed air, not wanting to believe that it was already so late.

In the canteen he could swallow nothing and felt more like vomiting; his colleagues gave him friendly advice to get some medicine at the infirmary. Too stupefied to realize that it would make him feel better, he did not get around to doing anything until two o'clock, but he had undoubtedly waited too long, because three pills barely eased his pain; his head was still cluttered with intermingled streaks and strands. All the same, he tried to get on with his office work, as he had to do the work of the absent Thomas at the same time as his own: the only result he achieved was a further confusion of the few strands of reason that remained to him.

At four o'clock he decided to return to the infirmary to see the factory doctor; he was told that he looked tired, but no alarming symptom was found: the doctor ordered him just to go home, to rest until the day after tomorrow and to take, if he felt like it, a tonic.

The streets were deserted, Boris found something abnormal and shocking in his presence in them; all the same, his migraine was a little better in the open air, becoming a confused buzzing in his head, feeling rather like a wad of cotton wool.

One after the other, people were coming out of hiding with strange expressions on their faces; it was easy to see that they didn't feel comfortable. Most of them, rather than walking in an ordinary way, moved themselves to only a few centimetres above the pavement with those uncertain motions of the legs which sometimes made them look as if they were flying, but were most of the time clumsy, ambiguous and probably useless. One wanted to make them sit down, but there were no benches in the narrow streets of the quarter. Nevertheless they gave the impression of being unable to stop themselves, their state of feeble agitation being permanent; at the same time they must have lost any memory of having one day been started on their journey and even more of the impulse which made them start. Their hands were another cause of worry, as if they did not know what to do with them; their swinging arms seemed to reach out to the right or the left as if to seize some invisible object always just out of reach, or else to draw, indicate or mark something in the air, but in vain: they left no trace except their shadows, and even they were doubtful, and in any case they moved with them.

Boris felt a certain lightness in his own gesticulations, which made him at each moment uncertain of the steps he was blindly taking forward into the void. Not being sufficiently conscious to take an interest in the manner of his progress, he walked on through the streets without any precise purpose, having, all the same, the vague impression that he was approaching home, but more by chance than by an effort of will.

At each moment that passed, he failed to recognize the houses around him; he also thought that he was lost, but without feeling the slightest discomfiture. Then, at the next crossing, he recognized where he was again and told himself that he had in no way strayed off the road, despite the little importance that attached to the matter. Perhaps he should be alarmed by his own indifference; today it all seemed to him merely comic, although the fact of finding himself on this route for no particular reason should make him fear that the reason was not a good one, or in any case that another one would do just as well.

"All roads lead to Rome," he told himself, almost aloud.

Once back in his room, Boris took two more aspirins and lay on his bed, but was unable to sleep.

It was only just dark. After tossing about for an hour, he ended up lighting the bedside lamp and taking the morning paper which he had already perused from the table. Newspapers had an incommensurate importance in his life: perhaps that proved he was losing his mind.

And yet, upon reflection he did not read any longer than usual; but he did so with more concentration as if expecting to find some revelation or marching orders. In fact, it was the only way in which he could get any information about the sovereign: there was always in practice an abundance of news items, more or less brief, about his public or private life. Without even realizing it, Boris would have liked to find in the columns some reflection of the preoccupations which had been troubling him since the day before; he could see nothing of the kind: neither plot, nor the beginning of an illness, nor an accident, not even a happy one; the King was, as always, in good health, smiling, out of reach.

Looked at another way, it was better like that. It would have been, so to say, at the expense of Boris's prerogatives if there had been the slightest variation from the norm, because he retained a proprietorial feeling for the man and suffered above all, as a consequence, at feeling that the life of the monarch was so little dependent on his own.

Certainly he had even seen the King, several times, if at a distance; he had never tried to get closer, and now suddenly he blamed himself for having neglected trying to do so. This King, who was *his own*, remained so much a stranger, so inaccessible, that he was no more than an abstraction, not even a symbol, in no way a human being; Boris began, as if it was quite natural, after some thought, to even doubt his existence.

Nevertheless his name appeared regularly in the pages: the King presiding over the first meeting of the new House, the King visiting the building works, the King receiving, opening, inspecting; all that put together did not add up to much of a life, even though the official dinners alone were enough to feed him.

One article, a little longer than the others, devoted to the performance which had just taken place at the Théâtre Royal, gave him a certain appearance of consistency: he appeared cheerful, jovial without any vulgarity, even rather sharp, and a good critic of drama, passionately fond, so it was said, of poetry, sometimes writing verses in the small hours. Boris, who ignored all these details, tried to distinguish between the truth and the flattery; but why was it necessary to flatter the King?

He tried to define the figure who passed in front of his eyes, seeing as of old a little man sitting up in an open carriage, still young-looking, with a pepper-and-salt beard and smiling eyes.

Even while he pursued it, the image loses its clarity little by little; soon nothing is left other than the shadow of a smile floating on the walls.

Boris, who has switched off the lamp, closes his eyes; the indistinct image continues to fade, with once in a while a flash of life in his look; his features keep changing, but freeze every so often into a series of grimaces which are sometimes grotesque and sometimes frightening...

Then it all calms down, but the head is farther away and at the same time larger; the enlarged eyes, although deeper set, are looking out with fear for something. Boris turns over in order to follow, from the other side of his view, the direction of the attentive eyes that seem to go straight through him in their brightness. Again he finds a landscape he knows, a stretch of fine sand interspersed with rocks and hollows along the seashore... The figure, more and more blurred, gradually disappears and is replaced by a confusion of piled-up rocks in the dim light of the falling night. Over there, on the crest of the dunes, a man moves away with rapid steps, his back slightly bent; an enormous black dog is running behind him.

Again a flat stretch, a heath this time, arid and stony, from which one cannot see the shore. The light is cold and sad, but seems to be that of the dawn.

I am tired, and my feet, which I no longer have the strength to lift, constantly stumble over the stones so that I risk losing my balance. I must have been walking for a long time and I am not sure of my bearings and exactly where I am: the ground undulates slightly with tufts of withered heather which sparsely cover the sterile soil, while stones sprout everywhere. Nothing clearly indicates where I am; I have the disagreeable sensation of being in an undifferentiated zone without any precise landmarks.

Nevertheless, I pursue my way in the hope that today I will find the tower; but will I recognize it in the gloom? Perhaps I have already passed it on my left or right with-out seeing it? Or else am I perhaps altogether in the wild, having lost all sense of direction? On our island nothing distinguishes one plain from another; indeed one often has the feeling that we could just as well find ourselves nowhere at all.

But in any case, I have no memory of such desolation as there is in this part of the island; so I must never have come this far before.

And then suddenly, after having climbed over a kind of barrier formed by piled-up shingle, I find myself on the beach in the middle of a stretch of fine sand, broken up by rocks and hollows, that has to be negotiated. The water is rising, with the waves coming suddenly together from many directions and mingling in dangerous eddies.

Once again at nightfall, at the seashore...

When Boris woke up again around seven thirty, he once again felt his headache of the previous day. He stayed in bed, as the doctor had given him a day off, but did not try to fall asleep again. Before his eyes, the smiling face with the little grey beard seemed to be waiting to be spoken to.

He had to do something. He had to penetrate into the King's inner circle by one means or another. Boris thought first of all of working as his valet or personal detective, but that would not be enough, it would be nothing compared to a real friendship. The amiable and brilliant talker seemed to be educated, intelligent and must also possess even more important qualities. In spite of the limited role that he was allowed to play in state affairs, it was always possible that he had a profound care for public affairs and that in the solitude of the White Palace he was looking for a real solution to the problems that seemed to exercise him so little. Perhaps he had found the right way to settle certain questions of state in which his entourage was all too interested – probably with less than pure intentions – in order not to have his own methods hindered. Boris, standing on the right side of his prince, would have joyfully worked at finding the happiest solution to a crisis that, at first sight, left little good to be expected; he would overcome, for *him*, the resistance of the ministers...

Alas, all that was impossible. Why did he have to choose the one person that a complicated and antiquated protocol separated from the rest of the world? The King, quite definitely, would remain outside his sphere. But was that not also the case with all the important men that he might want to reach? So there it was, there only remained assassination: death created a definite, and in a sense decisive, relationship. For someone who went about it diligently, it would no doubt be easy to carry out. The action could be accomplished by an ambush in some place where one knew the King would pass alone. The police took very few real precautions, as there was no motivation for anyone to bring about the end of such a monarch; the guards who circled the palace or stood at the official entrances were there more for appearance than for security, the soldiers in their ceremonial uniforms were as much a remnant of ancient times as the battlements of the castle. When he was on one of his private walks, anyone could walk up to him; but the problem in this case lay in the nigh on impossibility of being prepared for it in advance.

The best thing then was carefully to watch the public appearances which the newspapers wrote about in detail, from morning to night: it would therefore be judicious to read, systematically, all the information concerning matters of this kind. The occasion would present itself automatically.

Boris got out of bed, feeling much more relaxed now: the resolution he had just made had succeeded in calming his mind. He went out as quickly as he could in order to get the working materials he needed and passed most of the day in studying them.

He looked through the pages with a light heart, with the same concentration that would have gone into a visit to the King himself.

But in spite of this he made no discovery of particular interest, except that there was to be the inauguration of the "New Technologies Exhibition", which would take place the next day. There was a shortage of detail and, in any case, it was too soon for him to organize anything feasible. But then there was no hurry.

That evening Boris went to bed early and, feeling much better, slept immediately.

...Now that any turning back has become clearly impossible, the sand, rising gently towards the shore appears at last. With my limbs still shaking from having avoided all this violence, I climb the path that leads to the dune.

Now it is daylight, the sky is covered, the plain is entirely grey in the early-morning light. On a promontory two or three hundred metres away is a stone tower, square and crenellated; the windows are just loopholes.

I move forward, inspecting this place which I know so little, but which all the same has a reassuring appearance.

The tower is certainly very old; it seems to be in a bad condition. Now I remember having heard it talked about; an old legend had it that, once upon a time, it was inhabited by a hermit, living apart from others, about whom there existed countless rumours.

It is empty at present; only a few crows populate the old rooms; panicked by my approach, they fly up towards the sky through the crumbling arches.

The dilapidated stairway climbs up through the thickness of the outside wall itself, going several times around the edifice, up to its summit. The steps are broken, some have disappeared altogether; and then as it is very dark on this staircase, I can only move forward by taking endless precautions. In some places a piece of wall has even fallen in across the passageway, making the ascent even more difficult.

This climb is taking me even longer than I had expected. Here and there the steps are broken by Gothic arches giving a view of a series of corridors and rooms, larger and more numerous than one could have imagined from below; some of them are lit by a breach in the outer wall, others remain in cold and humid darkness.

I finally emerge onto what remains of a semi-destroyed narrow round platform. The view looks out over a landscape which is flat and featureless, the sea on one side, the land on the other, both dull and deprived of contour. What after all am I doing here?

I have climbed up here many times, always disappointed by the bleak landscape that awaits me. The mist is less thick today, one can see kilometres of sand and bush far away, becoming even more uniform by being seen from this height. I descend the well-known stairs, where the loose stones no longer conceal pitfalls from me. My head is light and at the same time confused after too little rest after a long insomnia.

It is time to return to the village: this morning I have to start working my field, where the ground is now ready, because it has not rained for several days. I must not fall behind.

The tower, seen from below, now looks far less high; it is only a feeble remnant of the immense construction that legend had placed there, a heap of stones little different from all the other heaps of stones strewn around the landscape. The brambles have invaded it and it is only with difficulty that one can recognize, leaning forward, a fragment of a pillar or some even less distinguishable architectural detail.

I continue walking along the seashore, crossing the funnels and piles of rocks, divided here and there by stretches of sand that make the going easier for a moment...

Little by little winter disappears. The weather has not changed very much in appearance, but we can all feel that a gentler mist caresses the ground. Although the sky is still covered, a warmer light bathes the land, where the green spears begin to appear on the withered boughs of the bushes. The seasons, the months, the years pass quickly. How short has been this winter that never seemed to finish!

On the sloping shingle of the bay we have pulled up our boats to get them ready to go back in the water. Marc and I are busy filling in, as best we can, the spaces that have grown between the flats with tallow mixed with tar.

We take our time; we caulk each opening with great care, while using as little as possible of the precious grease.

A few steps away, blond Eric is replacing a damaged plank; farther away the others are also at work, each one concerned with his own boat.

We can breathe the smell of the freshly turned earth, the result of our work, that sometimes overcomes that of the seaweed. The hawthorns at the top of the beach are already in flower; soon it will be spring.

Marc is quietly humming an old song that everyone here knows:

> To put the sea to sleep,
> Sing,
> Sing, sailor...

The words do not mean much; the tune is monotonous and slow, like a dirge; everyone sings it in his own way, so that the melody dissolves into a kind of prayer:

Sing, sailor.
The red gems
Will fill your nets tomorrow.
Less red is the song of the sailor,
Less strong is the hand that rows
Than the sand on the verge of tears
In the deep sleep of the sea.

Marc has stopped working; standing next to the boat, his stained hands hanging at his sides, he looks at the little round stones that roll under the waves. Eric is bringing down his hammer with a few oaths to spur him on, then he straightens up to examine his work.

...Less strong now your songs and your hand
Than the bitter red tears...

I like to hear these words which seem, although they have no meaning, to hide some mystery, some promise...

In spite of the concentration that I apply to my work, I have the feeling that I could do better; I go over the same parts, over and over again, without stopping, but without being fully satisfied: I tell myself that it is quite good enough to stop the water coming in, but can one be absolutely certain? And then, that's not the reason for it. I find myself dreaming of a beautiful boat, all of one piece, made of some hard but supple material which will never have a leak or a scratch... But how would we fill our days?

Sing, sailor,
Sing gaily,
Enchant until the morning
The deep sleep of the sea.

On Thursday Boris was back in his office, sitting at his desk, facing Thomas's empty chair. He had found his calculations of the day before yesterday in such a mixed-up state that he had to start all over again, but he was not making much progress; at each line he would raise his eyes from the page and look straight ahead, but without seeing anything.

The lines of an old ballad kept returning to his memory, with gaps that he was not able to fill in and words that he recited out of order.

The sailor sings while he rows, heavy is his heart and red are his hands. That wasn't right, neither the metre nor the words. *And he sings gaily to make death sleep.*

Suddenly an image comes to him: a beach full of stones where there are five or six fishing boats; men are at work around them; one of them, a little apart from the others, looks at the sea and sings...

Then nothing more.

6

EVERY YEAR AT ABOUT THIS TIME our bogs become full of insects, for the most part very small and light, so diaphanous, even insubstantial, that it is amazing they can live.

All they have are thin long legs, barely supporting transparent bodies, which hardly weigh anything at all, thin membraneous wings which the slightest breath of wind flutters, feathery antennae at the mercy of the slightest shock of the smallest drop of rain.

These insects signal to us, in place of any more obvious harbinger, the arrival of spring. We meet them in their millions, in great serried flights which tremble in the air, or else, like a fine dust, cover all the shrubs.

Hatching out in our swamps, they spread little by little all over the island. In the evening, when a window is left open, it is not long before their swarm invades the room. First of all you notice nothing, as each insect is so insubstantial; but then, to clear away the small spots in front of your eyes, you wave your hand; everything disappears. But just as quickly you find many more of them around you, disturbing the atmosphere, thickening the oil in the lamp or crackling in its flame. You wave your hand again, you blow, you blow harder; nothing ever does any good: the air becomes more solid, so compact is their flight, if you open your mouth you swallow hundreds of them; they penetrate your throat in their thousands.

Soon you have to give up the struggle; it is useless to close the window; it's already too late; the only thing you can do is to put out the light and take refuge in the heart of the night.

Their presence is less pervasive outside; they do not succeed in stopping your movements. Nevertheless you are aware of them everywhere, because some of them, through their bites which they can repeat a thousand times, pass on strange debilitating illnesses which keep us in bed, sometimes right through the summer season. As their stings are not painful and the beings that bite you are so little visible, it is difficult, if not impossible, to avoid them completely, and so we are always more or less bedevilled by the fevers they carry.

Some of these insects never leave the island pools which they cover like a mist; others stay on the surface. In the water itself there are bigger ones, thicker, more brightly coloured and also more repugnant in appearance, with brownish larvae which lie on the water plants, agile worms which change their shape as they wish, sometimes swollen like wineskins and sometimes tapering like needles, slow-moving dangerous insects that crawl in the swamp...

Yesterday I was leaning over a pool, looking for the bait that the fish find so appetizing, when I heard footsteps behind me. I did not turn round, thinking that it was one of my comrades, but suddenly I saw, beside my own reflection in the black water, the sombre eyes of the Hermit, shining. A water spider blown by the wind came to ripple the water for an instant, and once the surface was still again, he had disappeared.

I knew he had not moved away; I said without moving: "Who are you who follows my steps in front of me through the bogs and the dunes?" He did not answer right away, then, in a low but vibrant voice, replied:

"I am the one who comes with the dawn, the one whom one awaits before going to sleep, I am the star who guides a lost traveller in the night; I am the movement of the waves. I am in the blood of the lambs whose throats are cut, I am the pulp of the apple and the trunk of the apple tree. Here I am the one who looks at you..."

He went on, it seemed to me, for a long time, but I did not understand everything he said, and I have not retained any of it. It was both a reassurance and a cry of alarm, comparable to the song of the sea among the rocks.

When I could not hear him any more, I turned round: I saw no one.

The air was soft, almost without mist, a delicate scent of mint came up from the swamp. I moved forward among the new growing stalks, bent down to pick a few of the perfumed leaves and crushed them in my fingers. Above me, in the heavens a skylark cried out as it ascended.

Boris wandered over the soft earth which his footprints marked deeply, only to disappear immediately afterwards, so quickly did the elastic felt of the swamp recapture its normal shape. He tried to retrace his steps and his encounter of the day before.

But the tufts of peppered mint faded away, the pools no longer reflected the sky, the grey wall of Unit Eight was again framed in the window.

The page of calculations was lying on the desk, dry and unfriendly; a late fly was buzzing against the window panes.

Boris rose with the intention of killing it. The alcove was high and wide, the fly went from pane to pane, each time avoiding the too slow movements of its persecutor. Finally it made several noisy circles in the air and then settled on the frosted globe of the ceiling light.

Boris took a few indecisive steps and began to pull, one by one, the leaves off the day-to-day calendar which was fastened to the wall. It was Friday. Wednesday twenty-first, Thursday twenty-second, Friday twenty-third, St Bartholomew. Thomas had been gone for nearly a week. He himself had done nothing for two days; the work was piling up on the tables.

To tell the truth, the boss did not seem overly anxious to know the results he had requested: the statistical control of the factory seemed to operate half-heartedly most of the time, and the office responsible was a constant source of jokes among the other workers. But Boris and Thomas well knew that their chief often took a very active interest in the way things worked, saying that the manual labour seemed to him to be too slow, and he would then talk of using complicated machinery that would permanently control the assembly of the manufactured parts. It was not just a whim, because the same thing was happening in other factories. And then, over long periods, the two colleagues became so bored with their work that they were tempted to come up with any results at all, put together by chance, rather than pursue a task about which no one cared at all. But always there were scruples that stopped them in time: they could never be sure that the figures they assembled were not taken seriously in high places. And as it could always be said that the work made more sense when it was applied to a larger proportion of the manufacturing process, it seemed to them better to get on with it as far as was possible. In spite of all that, there were days of depression during which the calculators exchanged bitter remarks, complaining that they had little encouragement for their labours.

In the canteen, the news was circulating that the King was to visit the factory during the month of November. Boris, during the course of the afternoon, sat dreaming at his desk that the cortège would come to the end of the corridor and enter his office; he would receive a few discreet words of praise and some mention of the usefulness of the calculations that he made; the face with the little beard would smile, congratulate him with some flattering phrase, would perhaps give him some medal and then pass on, having consecrated the spot.

The whole thing was obviously absurd: the King would not even climb the stairs to the offices, would probably not even come to Workshop Z; the most important thing was to make him admire the new vertical-assembly machinery, which was in another part of the factory.

Boris went on with his work. The big blue fly had again started to negotiate the window panes.

After the long tramp through the corridors of the factory, surrounded by the troop of workers and other employees, Boris found himself back in the street. About to join the crowd waiting for the tram, he suddenly had a feeling of revulsion at the crush; after a moment's hesitation he rejected his impulse and decided to stay. Then, on further reflection, he decided that his new decision made no sense or at least had no importance, and wanted to leave after all, then once again he decided to stay, became confused over the indecision and finished by leaving anyway, because the tram was late in coming.

Without hurrying, he started to follow the metal rails on foot: it was the most direct route.

Passing a large stationer's, he moved around a rotating display of postcards and was struck by a photograph of a river, in a town, with a bridge in the middle and a few monuments visible in the distance. Boris asked himself what it was that had attracted his attention in this conventional view of a foreign town where he had never set foot: the picture had nothing interesting about it, artistic or otherwise, and as postcards went was rather blurred. Looking closer, he noticed that the camera seemed to have been pointed, not at the bridge – although it was the subject of the photograph as the caption confirmed – but at the paving stones in the foreground; while everything else was unclear, the paving stones which formed the quayside roadway at the bottom of the picture detached themselves with extraordinary clarity and seemed, so luminous were they, to be wet with rain. But the weather was absolutely fine.

Boris went into the shop, card in hand; the bell on the door gave out a clear ring.

There was no one inside, neither a salesperson nor a customer. All around him, down the side of the walls and up to the ceiling, drawers and pigeonholes were filled with so many different objects that they could have satisfied the most eccentric tastes. Boris suddenly had an inspiration, and when an old man dressed in a grey smock came in by a door at the back, he asked as naturally as he could if he had any photographs of the sovereign. The other made a grimace of surprise, indicating that the object was not often requested, thought a moment and, saying nothing, disappeared into the back of the shop.

The thought that the merchant had gone to telephone the police crossed Boris's mind, and he was tempted to take flight; but he persuaded himself with some difficulty that it was stupid. To divert his mind, he began to look at the shining paving stones on the quayside.

The man came back with a roll and asked him for what purpose he wanted this portrait. Taken by surprise, Boris stammered a few unintelligible words. The other, seeing his confusion, apologized: he had meant to say that he had no more in postcard size, nor in large reproductions, but only a photograph in colour, not very good and small in size – thirty centimetres by twenty approximately – that he now unrolled. It was on a very ordinary coated paper, printed in disastrous tints of purple and wine-red; the face itself had a curious lilac tint, the beard was like wine dregs. But the mischievous smile looked benevolent at first glance, if a little stiff, and the eyes were very alive. At the bottom of the print, in very small blue letters, one could read the word "Execution", followed by a star.

"That will do. I'll take it," said Boris. He paid for the postcard and the portrait, rolled up the latter, put the first in his pocket and left. The bells of the door tinkled gaily behind his back.

"That will do. I'll take it."

"The postcard too, sir?"

"Yes. What do I owe you?"

In spite of his efforts to think of something else, Boris could not get his mind off the few ordinary words he had exchanged with the shopkeeper. He had been going over them in detail for nearly five minutes since leaving the shop, automatically taking up the conversation from the beginning, from his arrival, up to the end, as if a record was stuck in his head.

"The postcard too, sir?"

Another look at the shining paving stones, swollen with moisture, at the side of the quay.

"Yes. What do I owe you?"

Looking for banknotes in his wallet, and then finding the change in the till which the little old man took an inordinate length of time to do... It was at least the tenth time that he had gone over the scene, which should normally have been incapable, it seemed to him, of holding his attention for more than a second. Irrevocably, as soon as he heard the bells ringing on his departure, he was once again on the doorstep of the dusty stationer's shop with the countless pigeonholes and it started all over again.

"Good day. Do you sell photographs of the King?"

The surprised look of the man in the grey smock... Boris tried to focus his attention on the front windows of the shops; but, looking at the books in the bookshop, the green ball of the chemist's, the bric-a-brac of the antiques shop, the exasperating record still went on playing.

Then suddenly the scene concentrated on the little sign which followed the word "Execution". The blue star now occupied all the space in his head, not like something of great importance which suddenly imposes itself, and of which the shattering discovery takes over all the faculties, but rather like the way a screen catches the light.

Boris blamed it on his mind-numbing office work. Perhaps he should give up this inept job to try something else? It was all a matter of chance; he could already see a long vista of streets in front of him, where his footsteps rang out, alone…

All the same, once he had arrived home, his decision was made: he would not go back to the factory.

I push open the door, the man from the tower is waiting for me.

The custom here is that no one locks the door of his house and everyone can go in everywhere; in spite of this advantage, we never go into each other's house: we have no reason to do so.

Malus is sitting on a stool next to the window, looking out at the bit of beach that one can see from there.

"Hello," he said, as if he were greeting me in his own home, and then in a deeper voice: "heavy tide this evening."

"Yes, I know," I answer, "everyone knows that." I am still standing by the door.

"Tomorrow," he goes on, almost as if talking to himself, "we will collect from the top of the shingle, at the last demarcation line of the seaweed, all the debris washed up from a world we will never see, driftwood sculpted into unknown forms, pieces of tackle twisted out of shape, stones smoothed out by the salt water or gem stones.

"Tomorrow we will find on the sand, between the broken urchins and the big mother-of-pearl seashells, stalks and grains and peelings: tonight the tide will wash up onto our shores useless plunder from the coasts of the earth…"

"What do you mean? Isn't our island part of the earth?"

"No. The earth is more beautiful, you know that. Over there are the flowers and the sun; in the shadow of the trees you can hear the song of the crickets…"

I interrupt him: "How do you know all that?" But he does not answer my question and goes on:

"In the middle of the night, when you wake in your solitary bed, you grope along the wall to find a warm and comfortable chair that will enfold you with its arms; but your hands only find the cold rough wall, and your stretching body tries in vain to fill the place of two bodies. It is the sad lot of the men of our island to live alone. Our reflective expression, the worried look that you see on our faces, are the marks of celibacy.

"Tomorrow the sea will wash up on our shores golden rings too narrow for any finger from here to slide through; wonderful jewellery will shine from the still-humid seaweed. Nobody will bend down to take them: such things represent no riches to us; to whom could we give them? Most of the men in the village could not even see them; even you, who would notice them, would give little heed to their brilliance; they would quickly tarnish as the stones dry and all the treasures collected would be no more by evening than a pile of little grey pebbles."

Boris looked at the photograph that he had just pinned to the wall with four drawing pins. One of the colours was slightly out of register in relation to the others, giving the whole picture the effect of a shaky rainbow. The figure had become more alive, his expression of benevolence – or rather of a well-meaning and familiar malice – was more noticeable. Boris remembered having read that morning of the games invented by the King to amuse his youngest son, doing what he could to compensate for the missing maternal tenderness.

On the other hand the beard looked false, as if it had been added as an afterthought; in any case the King had let it grow longer since his wife's death.

Boris regretted not having gone to this exhibition, in order just to see it, out of goodwill; he did not even know if he would have recognized the officials in the crowd; and then again it was interesting to see how this kind of ceremony would unfold, and how it might be possible to approach the procession.

The man looked at Boris as if he was guessing his thoughts. It seemed that his ironic expression had become more pronounced: in the shop his face had seemed to be more closed, more conventional. Perhaps this was because of the white border which he had cut off (with the little star), or because of different lighting? He would find out in the daylight.

Boris moved backwards, sat down on his bed, directly facing the portrait; the look was at present fixed on the wall behind him or on something even farther away. The smile was fixed, looking more like a grimace, like someone who had just noticed the barrel of a firearm pointed towards him.

Without taking his eyes off the photograph, Boris undressed and got into bed after turning off the overhead light. The facial expression became more pronounced, and at the same time the eyes began to shine with an unbearable brilliance, certain to take into the tomb with them a truth that no one would know… Boris turned his head away.

And then a kind of laugh was heard, shaking the air of the room as if an army had invaded it. The portrait grew in the dim light, the eyes burned like headlamps, the mouth opened to speak…

Boris got up as calmly as he could, went to look more closely at the picture, caressed its surface with his fingers; it was supple and smooth. The bottom-right drawing pin was not exactly at the right angle. He carefully withdrew it, and put it back to the left, a little… then a little more… then suddenly moved it by several centimetres, and suddenly pushed it into the middle of the uniform, between the ribbons and medals, approximately where the heart was.

Then he turned out the bedside light, slipped between the sheets and turned his head towards the wall.

7

MALUS CAME LAST NIGHT and again spoke to me about the earth. Where did he learn these things? He could doubtless not have gone there himself, because how could one imagine, finding himself there, that he would not have stayed? It was already late when I heard a knocking on the downstairs door, the one that looks out to sea. I opened it: his eyes were as bright in the darkness as those of predatory birds, while everything within him seemed to be consumed by a flame that is unknown among us.

When he entered he said nothing, but he seemed to be carrying within him such a powerful sense of elation that at that particular moment I would have preferred him not to have come all this way down to here; at the same time I could no longer not wish to keep him here. He sat next to the chimney, where a few potatoes were baking beside the coals. We ate them together with some dried fish, without exchanging a word. Then, turning towards the fire onto which we had piled more logs, he began to talk in his low, monotonous voice, which sometimes flared up with sudden heat.

"On the mainland," he said, "so far inland that you can no longer smell the odour of seaweed mingled with the wind of dusk, there are forests which stand so high that their trunks, lined up like a marching army, are lost in the clouds and the sky, forests that cover whole counties and are so vast that those who get lost in them will never find their way out. But the clearings, which are all covered with new grass, some-times give the traveller a sight of the sky. Look! At the foot of the tree trunks, as wide as towers, brilliantly coloured flowers grow, purple butterflies flutter around, looking for the perfumed sugar on which they intoxicate themselves; up there in the rustling foliage, golden birds are shining, singing, to the point of madness, to the glory of the world.

"Can you hear the song of the birds? Can you hear them laugh as they play and the explosion of their delight?"

But all I heard was the crackling and the hissing of wood which was still too green.

"On the mainland," he went on, "so far away inland that you can see neither seaweed nor seagull, there are cities where the dazzling high buildings, grouped close together, rise up in giant clusters, immense cities where, for days and weeks on end, you only come up against steel and stone. But through the prisms of glass or concrete shines the tree of light. Look at them! Between the walls, a hundred storeys high, run the lighted streets, millions of pedestrians hurry along them towards the work which summons them; they hardly have time to glance at the altars on which they are offered the greatest splendour in the world.

"Can you see the abundance of diamonds that are everywhere on offer? Can you see the amber lights and the ripe fruits in their baskets?"

But all I could see were the embers and the blackened wood in the grate.

"Over there," he continued, "so far into the interior that you can no longer hear the sound of the sea, shines the love of men…"

And so the reddened coals shaped themselves into continents with all their outstretched plains, where the cultivated fields and the orchards of the earth ripened, where the rivers ran and birdsong surges from the fountains. The strident fanfares of trumpets suddenly rose from the flaming logs.

Yes, I can smell the flowers, I can hear the laughter, I can see the cities, I can inhale the water of the rivers. I see the blood and I believe you, because you are the madman of this kingdom. Under your orders a war fleet advances, ploughing through the lagoon and the undergrowth with its bows, hollowing out the hills and valleys, while, behind, the young corn, germinating in its wake, covers the mirror of the days with its trembling green.

Yet, in the heart of the capital itself, it is night. Anxious foreheads lift themselves up from the pillow, waiting for the return of the sun; it has been night for far too long.

At all the crossroads of the forest, the signals are blocked at red; without pausing, the traffic rolls on in all directions, a low rhythm of sounds, resembling a tom-tom. Strident whistles smash the bodies of the drivers, piercing lungs and skulls. A rat caught in a trap suddenly smells its fear, like a watchtower in the middle of barbed wire, but the worried paw that it wants to pass over its muzzle feels nothing underneath, and it has no more eyes to see its severed head, which looks back at it a few yards farther on, amazed at the body that had supported it for so long.

In the heart of the capital, a sudden tornado brings down sections of the walls with a single gust, and the water runs down over the fresh plaster, carrying everything away with it. From the very top of the highest skyscraper I look down at the flotsam which is being carried away by the current of rubbish. I am an old vulture whose wings can no longer carry him; and I stay motionless, my head bent, looking all the way down to a point amid the crowd, an empty point which is passing by and which is me.

Malus is still there in the room, fast asleep from fatigue in his chair; his head has grown considerably bigger and now almost occupies the whole room; the fire is dead, the little air which remains has become unbreathable. In the darkness, striped with white dawn light, we can hear the distinct clamours of words that are clearly articulated, but of which the meaning escapes us. In the midst of the familiar faces we take off, my vulture on my shoulder, Malus carrying his head under his arm, without rudder or compass, over waters uncharted on any map. The black flag floats over us.

We sail slowly through the ruined town, where the fires started by the storm have put themselves out. The scorched earth lies on our right and to our left, covered with twisted metal. The landscape has no surprises, and we too lie down on the bridge to catch a little dreamless sleep.

On waking, I am alone on the surface of the sea, in a light that seems under threat, as on days of eclipse. How long have I been asleep? The water and sky, equally still and frozen by the calm, crush my boat with their weight; it is impossible to move forward or even to know what direction to take. I do not know how many hours, perhaps even years I have waited here, without any movement, hoping for a breeze.

Here and there large flat blocks of ice are floating, lustre-less and heavy, left here by some current that had brought them from the ice floes and, suddenly discouraged, they look like the white birds of which we sometimes find the corpses, who die of boredom before they are able to reach their journey's end.

I did not bring any provisions for the journey, and my feeble state is becoming extreme; but having no appetite I do not suffer from hunger, and as for thirst, the stale water on which I float is at least drinkable.

My travelling companions have probably awakened a long time before and, gripped by idleness, had let themselves slide, silently, without regret, without even thinking about it, overboard.

Half-asleep, one throws an arm overboard that is allowed to float loosely in the lukewarm water, slowly, abandoned; overtaken little by little by this languor, the body passes insensibly from the breathable air to the water of death. One finds oneself already in it completely, a single hand still holds the boat, the water rises up to the mouth that opens by itself, to attempt, before the end, a feeble smile. The arm lets go; there is perhaps still time to save oneself. But to what purpose? The water enters the nostrils, already the throat is filling.

This is how, one by one, my sleeping friends disappeared; the last glance they gave to those still on the boat was no doubt an appeal: not an appeal for help, but one invitation to bliss.

I myself must have fallen asleep, in spite of myself: as I regain consciousness, I notice that the waves have become stronger; and looking around I see that we are approaching a coast, a low coast that one can just make out on the line of the horizon.

Soon the land becomes clearer: what had started off as a thick mist, lying on the water, can now be seen to be a clear stretch of sand with, above it, a line of green. On the right a group of houses can be seen; then there is an elevation of the land, like a cliff, which rises there. It must be a headland sticking out, or else perhaps an island.

A plank passes nearby, which I quickly seize to use as an oar to make more progress.

Yes, this land is an island, I recognize it: it is the same one where I have passed all my life, this sand is that of the big bay, these few houses are those of our village. I bring myself nearer with vigorous strokes of the oars.

Maur and Marc did not come out with me this morning. All alone I did not catch many fish.

That night Boris slept badly; towards the morning he had a nightmare. He had turned up at the office together with Thomas, but it was in the country, among the meadows and fields. The more they advanced, the more doleful the country became, and it ended by being no more than a plain without tree or vegetation. Thomas described his "accident" with all kinds of useless details, overly precise circumstances, which sounded as if they had been badly invented, so numerous and petty were they. He could not, in all likelihood, have remembered so much from the few minutes which preceded the shock. He must have gradually imagined the whole thing, which appeared to fascinate him. He therefore went on, without being aware of it, relating what had happened before and after the collision, although he had lost consciousness at the time.

As Boris did not reply, the other ended up staying silent; at this moment they were passing in front of an isolated enclosure where horses were fenced in, four red horses standing rigidly on their hooves; their heads raised in an attitude of anxiety, they seemed afraid of being surprised by some important event of which the imminence was not in doubt.

They both increased their step. They then met a farmer who asked them if they had seen the horses. They answered that they had seen them, and Thomas added naively that perhaps it would be better to "explain it all to them". "Explain what to them?" said the peasant with a surly voice. "There's nothing to be explained to them."

They entered a village where there was some feverish activity going on: men and women were rushing around the houses, pushing their children hastily inside, closing the windows, barricading the shutters and the doors as best they could. Boris wanted to ask the cause of all the tumult, but he found only unfriendly faces in front of him that seemed in no way inclined to engage in conversation. Nevertheless someone said to them as they passed: "You would do better to find a shelter: the horses are coming." Without even giving them the time to answer, the man pushed his door shut; they could hear him inside, turning the keys in the lock and pulling the heavy bolts.

Boris walked faster; he could already hear a galloping rhythm approaching.

At the next group of farms, not very far away, all the doors were closed and the outside shelters padlocked. A clamour could now be heard, mounting from behind the walls; all of a sudden a voice shouted, very clearly, very close by: "There they are!" then threw out a cry, like someone being beaten to death. Boris looked at Thomas: in his place was a deformed being, with two scrawny legs and a horse's head, which was braying with all its teeth, while dilating its nostrils. Boris began to run, when the animal opened its mouth and began to whinny in a horrible manner.

He woke up in a heavy sweat, turned over in bed and as quickly fell asleep again.

A sheer cliff stretches from this part of the island from our village up to the northernmost point, dominating the sea in places from a height of a hundred or so metres. A few rare indentations interrupt it, giving issue to five or six little sandy coves; all the rest is only an abrupt rampart of granite and shale, fringed with gigantic rocks with their jagged contours that the winter winds have torn from the coast.

A violent wind is always blowing on the coastline. Even in summer the sea is constantly agitated; it throws itself furiously against the outer reefs, splashing back in great bouquets, forming sheets of moving froth, while retaining enough spirit to strike the very side of the cliffs, gradually eroding its walls, penetrating into its irregularities, roaring and gurgling in unpredictable ways.

It is in this way that the sea has hollowed out a complicated system of tunnels and grottos which mine the coast in depth; and the walker hesitates to go too near the edge, as with his weight alone he risks seeing a whole section of rock crumble under his feet. To tell the truth, accidents of this kind are not very frequent, so that we often tend to forget the danger.

I am sitting next to Malus on a grass-covered bank which overhangs from high above the violence of the waves. With our eyes we follow their arrival and their retreat, and the unexpectedly eddying currents in the enclosed basins between the rocks. A yellow or red froth rises at the heart of the whirlpools and is blown away in bubbles by the wind. We are quiet: amid the uproar of the elements it is almost impossible to be heard. The north-easterly wind, however, is so strong that it dulls the face and the senses, paralysing the lips, making the eyes water, contracting the forehead and freezing the thoughts.

But my companion begins to articulate his words into the face of the tempest; and it seems as if the disorder around us has died down, so smoothly do the words slide through the murmuring of the wind and the waves.

He speaks of the sun, of the coming summer; attentive gulls hover over his words. He is talking about the harvesters and the sharp cries of the crickets are mingled with his voice. He is speaking of wonderful peaches and of flocks of golden fleeces: the song of the herdsmen rises from above the pastures full of flowers.

He talks of the heat of the afternoon and of resting under the fig trees, of being thirsty and drinking the cold water of the springs...

The wind redoubles its force, the sea batters the wall of the cliff with great blows. I am alone facing the ocean, the clamour ravishes my ears, the hurricane throws the burning spray in my face.

He talks of gentle fertile valleys and of rural festivals: on the nights of the wine harvest we drink the new wine which flows from the press, and then we sleep, drunk, where we lie in the white arms of the washerwomen.

"Soon we shall see the July schooners crossing the shining sea. Majestically, they will come to drop anchor in the shelter of our reefs; our harbours will swarm with coloured men with singing voices who will unload their cargoes here; bundles of precious cloth, jars of oil, baskets of fruit and spices will pile up on our quays, while a thousand joyous cries will ring through even our narrowest alleyways.

"The summer is returning with long days and hot nights; already the season of the gladioli has arrived; soon the sirens will be born again.

"On the steamy beaches, in the hollows of the rocks, we will find gold-skinned young women, rapid and supple swimmers, with hair like undulating seaweed.

"They are the daughters of the sea spray, sired by the sun on the crest of the waves, and their laughter, which never ceases, soothes the greatest sorrows. We will dance reels with them on the sand, we will decorate their bodies with necklaces of mother-of-pearl and dresses made of kelp that we will create for them, then we will go to rest among the dunes and we will hold in our hands the valleys and the thickets of the sky.

"Your youth," he went on, "tells you that my words are unreasonable; but then your eyes, already fixed on the horizon, look down to see what is closer, your step gets shorter, falling in step with another's, your arm goes around a waist, your mouth gets softer; you are already awaiting the one who is coming for you, your lover who tastes of salt..."

Our bad weather is of short duration, and we quickly forget the sadness of the winter months.

8

T HE SITUATION HAD BECOME clearer since the beginning of September. The King, having tried several times to reach the usual compromises, in despair before the obduracy of the Church, had given his assent to government that did not include them. But this initiative also failed because of the abstention of one of the other groups; so it was necessary to accept the conditions of "the strongest party". The Church, although it wanted to avoid a public row, still insisted from the beginning that it had to occupy the principle levers of command: so it was given the ministries of the Interior, of Public Works and of Information, as well as a few secondary posts. It realized that more extensive demands would run the risk of pushing its different enemies into a coalition.

Public opinion, and it was above all there that the real change could be seen, was interested to a certain extent in these manoeuvres. A certain popular movement, as Laura had predicted, could be observed and, in spite of the methods used – which were dubious to say the least – a first step forward seemed to be well and truly on its way.

Action published a special edition every day, which was filled with colour photographs, the novelty of which attracted attention. On Saturday afternoon and on Sunday, the Church organized sporting events and big public musical-hall spectaculars for the benefit of the voters, in order to celebrate its success, according to the party. Entry was free for everyone and an immense crowd gathered. From time to time, once the audience was well warmed up, a loudspeaker announced the latest political developments, as if these were the principle concern of the spectators, who came to the conclusion on that account that such information must interest them in the extreme, as otherwise no one would go to the trouble to communicate it in the very middle of their entertainment. The more sober and reflective among them only resisted being convinced with an effort, hesitating each time they heard a dubious new proclamation being delivered with such enthusiasm by a celebrated boxer or a champion cyclist.

On the Sunday evening there were great rejoicings in celebration of the government which had just been formed, with parades, balls and fireworks.

Boris, who had spent the whole day in his room, read all about it the following Monday. In spite of his decision on Friday, he had returned to the factory the next day by force of habit, and had done the same that Monday; he disliked himself for this weakness, reproaching himself for having too little follow-through in his ideas and being thereby responsible, without knowing why, for the fairground triumphs that the Church Party was bringing home.

He was in a bad mood. During the morning he had encountered the Hermit wandering about the cliff, but had only obtained vague and reticent words from him. The other seemed to have little memory of his inflammatory declarations of the day before: when asked for an explanation, he said that he had probably been feverish, even going so far as to talk of an attack of marsh fever. Boris had also wanted to know why he did not live in the village like everyone else; this question really seemed to surprise him: he answered that he had not even known there was a village, that otherwise he would certainly have lived there, because his tower was in no way comfortable and the constant proximity of the sea was in the long run irritating. Yes, of course he was always looking at it: he had no choice, because there was nothing else to look at.

Irritated, Boris, not knowing what to expect, ended by asking him if the sirens would be coming soon. But there too he received only confused answers: there were no sirens, nobody believed in these children's stories. Who was there who could say that he had ever seen a single one?

They separated, each irritated with the other.

Even though the alarm had not gone off, Boris woke from sleep at the usual time. He stretched his arm out towards the bedside table and turned the big round clock to face the other way so that he would no longer have to see it. The tick-tock was louder than ever.

Boris tried hard not to hear it by putting his head under the covers with one ear glued to the pillow, the other carefully covered by the blanket. It was no good. Giving up, he sat up in bed, picked up the clock, and having looked at it for a good minute, unscrewed the back with a nail file which was near at hand. The little cogs turned without difficulty, all together but at different speeds; a slight dizziness stopped him from looking elsewhere.

After a while Boris felt the cold on his shoulders; then he delicately fitted the nail file into the machinery, blocking the balance wheel, then put it down again on the table. But sleep did not return.

He got up again and without thinking removed the nail file, the angle of which did not fit in with his idea of harmony.

The tick-tock continued with its regular beat and the hands began to move again. Had they stopped for a whole hour or only for a few minutes? It was very annoying not to know and, to make matters worse, his wristwatch hanging from its nail had stopped at midnight, because it had not been wound up.

Boris got dressed and went out. The concierge, as he passed her lodge, said to him, instead of good morning, "Well, we're not very early today, are we?" Which was true enough; he was not early. Not knowing what to reply, he automatically moved towards the tramway stop, where he bought his newspaper.

The meeting of the Council of Ministers, the report of the proceedings in parliament, the ten-point programme of the Church; Boris had had enough of all that and turned the page.

The first communion of Prince Jacques, with details of the "grandiose ceremony" that was to accompany it; this was without any question another of the party's inventions. The royal family's weekend in the country; among the guests were a high proportion of members of the Church or of its fellow travellers. The King appeared to be very much in a hurry to play the game of these adventurers; it was highly improbable that he could sincerely go along with their schemes, and it was more likely that he gave way through cowardice. He was already nearly dead: he could be finished off easily.

Little Jacques would become an orphan, which was very sad, even though one did not know if in reality he loved his father or not; but in any case his future was assured. There was in fact no chance that a simple regicide would bring about a total change such as a revolution, even a palace revolution. Even the possibility of a change of dynasty lay only in the realm of the imagination. But that was no reason to forgo an act that remained the only way to bring matters to an end.

"On 18th September, the King will visit an interesting innovation that the General Factory has just introduced…" That is when the crime would take place. Boris managed to concentrate his attention on the article, which he had already read from beginning to end several times. He knew all about the new assembly plant and its surprising new units. The King would have to follow the assembly line, then take one of the lifts to go down again, floor by floor. And then, apart from the goods lift, only one of them descended to the hall of the main entrance; it was certainly that one the officials would take and, given the limited capacity of the cabin, they would take it one by one, with the King leading.

All that had to be done then was to wait for the victim at the intermediate stop in the dark corridors of the building, to stop it in motion with the help of the push button, and then to get the job done. After that he could send the body in one direction or the other...

On the main stairway there is a crowded throng: at such a moment everything is quite different from the usual scene. Workers and engineers are hurrying, going up to the reception room on the top floor, or else going down after adding a last touch to the stage or to the lighting or the welcome banners. Journalists and photographers carrying their equipment can also be seen.

On the third floor several corridors branch off in different directions, and the narrowest one leads to the target; it is empty and marked "No Exit" right from the beginning. Boris goes down it.

Once past the bend one is completely out of sight. The little door is there and everyone knows that it can be opened by every key. Boris, like the others, has often occupied himself by opening it and making clandestine visits there during the lunch break, thanks to the easy-going watchman. This time too he comes to the end of the corridor silently, opens the door carefully, and slides through it into the darkness. Nobody has seen or heard anything at all.

Once his eyes have become a little acclimatised, he can make out the vague outlines of the objects around him; a faint glow comes from the cage of the lift at the far end. Boris goes towards it.

This corridor, which was only ever intended for potential maintenance works, is in fact so encumbered with the most varied number of objects that it can only be penetrated with great difficulty: every size of packing case is piled up to the ceiling, packets of metal tubing and angle plates litter the floor; everything that could get in the way of the cortège must have been piled up there in haste, which would explain the disorder.

Boris arrives at the rectangular platform, suspended in the middle of a skeleton of pipes and bolts which hold up the edifice; at the far end is a hole, which is where the lift cabin passes through. All he has to do is wait: the first person to come through it will be the King. Otherwise it will be a failure, a risk that has to be faced. On the panel the different buttons are easy to recognize in the gloom: this one stops the lift and this one controls the light, so that the victim can clearly see his assassin.

Boris has only just, with difficulty, made them out when he hears a click down below and the sound of the motor running. The time has come.

The cabin rises very slowly with a rather unpleasant noise that reminds one of the dentist's drill. Boris takes the kitchen knife with the very sharp blade that he has brought with him from the inside pocket of his jacket, carefully takes the paper wrapping off it, and puts this latter into his side pocket. Already the top of the little box has appeared at the edge of the platform.

He gets ready; all the same his heart is beating a little faster than normal, his hand approaches the stop button. With everything in the right position, he presses it. The cabin instantly stops but the motor goes on running, which is better for him. At the same time the light goes on and the door onto the corridor is opened: the smiling face with its little beard is there and looks out with an astonished expression.

He has to act quickly. Boris strikes, then rapidly withdraws his arm and stays stupefied as if he had just received the blow himself... The light goes out, the door closes again with an abrupt slam. The lift has continued its ascent. He has probably pressed the button with his other hand without realizing it; the knife is still in his right one, the blade hardly stained. He wraps it again in the paper he has taken out of his pocket, taking good care not to leave any piece of it behind as "evidence".

Then he gropes his way towards the exit corridor, saying to himself several times over: "I've plenty of time, plenty of time."

I can hear them, I can hear their song, so soft that it is confused at first with the sound of the wind in the long grasses of the dunes. They are not there yet, but in two or three days, perhaps tomorrow, I shall see them, in the reality of their warm living flesh, engaged in drying and combing their long hair, tangled by the winter, in the hot sun. We often believe that the sirens are monstrous beings, neither women nor fish, who have tails instead of legs. Those who repeat the fable have certainly not seen them walking along the shore or dancing on the sand with their agile limbs, their narrow waists, their little breasts, slender necks and long silver hair.

Tomorrow we shall see them emerge from the folds of the waves, fluttering their eyelashes and shaking the fine droplets of shining water from their shoulders; some of them will amuse themselves by staying in the sea and swimming in the waves, laughing with pleasure, while the others begin to dance in graceful circles.

Then, mingling our songs with theirs, we shall slowly approach their magic circle and side by side with them we shall dance the routine of the ritual figures and then, lying next to them on the fine sand, we shall teach them to speak the language of men.

Boris, without wanting to, quickened his pace. Stumbling between the planks and the metal bars, he moved nervously through the narrow passage which now seemed interminable on his return. Then he reached the little door that he had not quite closed; a little daylight filtered through the length of the passage. As he heard no suspicious sound on the other side he pushed the panel open and found himself in the corridor leading to the principle staircase. A quick look at his hands, then at his clothes: everything looked normal and unstained. The body should not yet have arrived at the top; he had no need to hurry.

His breathing having become normal again, he calmly negotiated the corner. The crowd was less dense, but his arrival went totally unnoticed by all the people coming and going through the other corridors. He started to go down the stairs...

As he reached the ground floor, an uproar could be heard coming from the upper floors: something had just happened, but he did not know what it was. Around him the onlookers began to ask others what is happening, but they did not know either. He broke away from the mob, which was growing minute by minute in front of the entrance to the building and continued on up the avenue.

The paper gave a few more details about the future visit, as well as the different itineraries that the sovereign would, so it was said, follow in the provinces. He really gave himself unstintingly, he whom one normally saw so seldom; the Church manipulated him cunningly, from the opening of public works to solemn masses, giving on the one hand a new popularity to the monarch, and on the other an official character to all its own ceremonies, the popularity of the former rebounding, in the end, on the party. He was only a pawn, a simple pawn in the propaganda of the party; his sympathetic "salt of the earth" persona was both publicity and a fallback for the party.

All this added up to the strategy which Laura had explained: the increasing assimilation into the government of the private policies of the Church.

In the same way, although no law had been voted through, the subject had not even been raised in the House, one could see nevertheless that the restoration of the old cathedral of Retz, having been started years ago and carried on with customary slowness, was now being raised to the level of a national campaign. And it was announced, as a matter of course, that the King would soon come to visit the site.

No one claimed that any kind of resolution had been taken in this sense: the interminable discussions that constituted the principle subject of disagreement between the different groups were simply pushed aside, and those who had hardly understood them could now believe in good faith that the Church's project had finally won over all the others, as at least a start had been made. Every supposition was permissible as to when the decision had been made, because not only was it at least three years since the rebuilding of the basilica had officially started, but no one could say precisely whether that constituted the true starting point of the works.

And on top of it all, the King was covering up the scandalous confusion with his presence. Such a willingness to cloud the issue was in any case a bad omen for the party that had declared its intention to "appeal to all sincere people". It was a curious sincerity that started off by manipulating the time scale. Laura would undoubtedly want to say: "appeal to all credulous people". The Minister of Public Works belonged to the party, which was proof enough: the others closed their eyes and the King's sly little smile gave absolution.

I shall walk along one of the interminable sectors of the western coastline with the tide going out, where, for miles and miles, not a single rock interrupts the monotony of the sandy strip that stretches ahead out of sight between a flat dune, covered with tamarisk shrubs, and a sea that is flatter still.

As is my habit, I shall walk, not far from the water, at this place where the sand, still wet, is reasonably firm under my step, looking down at little orange or pink rocks strewn around my feet, picking up the prettiest ones from time to time, only to throw them away again almost as quickly without a qualm, because the beach is covered with them and the ones I hold in my hand quickly lose their shine.

Tired of this game, I shall raise my eyes to see if the most distant point is as far away as ever, knowing perfectly well that on the other side of it is another stretch of shore in every respect similar to this one. But ahead of me, I shall see instead a slender silhouette, too alluring to belong to an inhabitant of the island, coming along the beach towards me. We shall slowly approach each other, she a little lower on the beach than I am, walking just alongside the waves. Soon we shall only be separated by the distance between our two paths; she will stop looking at the water which is rapidly hollowing out the sand under her heels.

In a low voice, I shall call her name, "Aimone… Aimone…"
Then, having crossed these few metres with measured steps,
I shall draw her gently towards me. Then the last clouds will
flee to the four corners of the sky, the sea will draw back its
waters into the distance, and from the dunes, in flower at
last, the intermingled perfumes of the carnations and the
evergreens will drift down towards us.

I shall take the hand of my friend, together we shall climb
the sandy rise and we shall walk past the first row of thistles,
behind which another one lies a little higher and, behind
them, a third one higher still. But on the other side of the
third dune, surmounted in its turn, we shall enter the happy
valley, the wide, fertile valley that will display for us its fields
of alfalfa and oats.

It is hot and the air is full of the humming of threshing
machines. Under the apple trees, in the dust of the road,
the fallen fruits are rotting while giving off a slight odour of
cider. Waving hedges, walls whitened with lime, tiled roofs;
from farm to farm the roosters are answering one another.

At the bottom of the valley a river flows majestically and
we are going towards it; moored next to a wooden bridge,
a little barge is waiting for us, filled with sweet-smelling
supple straw. When we climb into it, the rope that holds

it detaches itself and we float away, carried by the current under the passive eyes of the big tan-coloured cows.

On each side poplar trees, with their shadows stretching across the prairie, pass us by on the banks. The day is already over. The hills that we saw a little while ago have grown apart and have become blurred in the distance.

The landscape has very quickly lost its vivacity, the houses seem farther apart, the herds of animals are harder to see. Now we are going through a grey plain, almost uncultivated and stripped of trees, with large semi-deserted empty spaces. The flat banks pass by slowly, indistinct, muddy. Finally the barge, through an accident of the current, stops among the reeds.

I get off at a bank covered in yellowish silt, and automatically reach out my hand to help someone to follow me; there is no one there. A name that had come to my lips escapes me as well, disappearing into the mist. Walking along the estuary swamps, I get back to the coast.

Without knowing how, Boris found himself in front of his house; so then he started to climb the steps that lead to his room.

9

For more than two weeks my friend Malus has hardly ever left me. We pass whole days together, lying on the rocks above the sea, listening to the sound of the waves.

The weather is fine, the wind brings an already sweet and tepid breeze to our faces; there are only a few small white clouds left, very high in the sky, and they float over the island without stopping. All around us the heather is in flower and is humming with thousands of bees; furtive lizards glide over the stones, stay still for a long moment, then cover one or two metres at incredible speed only to freeze again suddenly, turning their heads to look for who knows what and give imperceptible darts of their tongues into the open air.

The catch is abundant, the lambing has proceeded without problems; the very little work that we have to accomplish in the fields is greatly helped by this dry season. We keep ourselves busy during the long hours of leisure by warming ourselves in the rays of a sun which is stronger every day than the day before; and every evening we return to the village and we can read, in the redness of the setting sun, a sign that tomorrow will be even better.

"Doesn't it seem to you," Malus said to me today, "that we can see a wedding dress shining for an instant in the hollow of the waves and unkempt ringlets of hair through their perforated folds? Doesn't it seem to you that the water moves in even more harmonious curves?"

In turn I asked him, "Why don't the sirens stay on our island all year long?"

"They once lived here, but in our climate they quickly become mortally bored; they rapidly lose their gaiety and their splendour on our mist-ridden isle. Do we not love them better that way? And are we not always with them? Have we not followed them often enough in our minds in the long humid nights and through the monotonous uncertainty of winter? Do we see anything other than their arms in the branches of the trees, than their eyes in the pools of water, their mouths in the purple flames of the peat? And at night, lying on our backs, we still watch the curves of their bodies on the lines of the ceiling beams."

"Tell me, can it be that our thoughts can be somewhere else? Their cry, their strange cry, will it never leave us, or will it just happen some day that we shall not hear it any more, so full are our ears, and shall we, with the same forgetfulness, confuse it with the deep call of the ocean?"

"Tomorrow you will go towards her, but ever since the beginning she has been with you."

The sea is low. It has retreated so far with these great tides that one has the impression of being able to walk from the village to the opposite point by cutting straight across the immense empty bay; the whole stretch of polished sand gleams in the sunlight, and with such force that you can barely open your eyes. One hardly dares to proceed alone across the shining mirror.

But Aimone doubles my imprinted footsteps with the lighter ones that her bare feet leave in the sand; and I too am light, knowing she is next to me.

From time to time I carry her, slender and laughing in my arms, so that she can avoid the stretches of painful gravel that she cannot jump over, or else when she is afraid of slipping on the patches of purple clay, perforated by piddocks.

Farther on, we walk side by side over fine sand, spangled with mica, on which the sea has just left pools which run out into a network of hundreds of little rivulets, leaving at risk the tiny soles which cling to them.

Still farther away, past the zone of hairy stones where the little crabs hide, we come to the slightly milky water of the sea-grass beds. There we proceed a little more nervously: so many little rapid touches, contacts that sting or cling, make one wary of more dangerous encounters; there are long green strands which wrap themselves around the legs and froth that one raises at every step, which make it difficult to see anything at all, except for the sudden viperous flight of some sea snake.

During the time that we are haphazardly advancing, picking up black clusters of cuttlefish eggs and capturing sea horses, the water has become deeper. Once it has reached our knees, we turn to the right in order to get back to solid land on the other side.

Once again we pass a few stones covered with algae and hollows of tepid water where the starfish dream; then once more the firm sand, strewn with shells that stretch their pink tongues into the outer air...

Finally, tired out, we walk back towards the shelter of the dunes.

At the top of the beach, Aimone stretches herself out in the sun; as for me, I rock her and kiss her as I talk to her. She only laughs, understanding few of the words that I decline and conjugate for her. "I love you, Aimone, Mona, the only one. Aime, almond, anemone of the shining skin; silver eyes, smiling mouth. My own soul, my lovely Aimone.'

I embrace her languorous, weary heart, which softly returns my caresses; smooth, loving, complaisant, a little nervous. A golden creeper with indolent and undulatory movements, Aimone the beloved, a defenceless sea craft, daughter of the sand and the sea froth, born from my body and lying in the depth of my sleep.

Do you know, gentle shadow disappearing into the sunset, do you know when you return, how longingly I have waited for you?

From the top of the dune, I follow at a distance the line of the sea that closes the bay. For the first time, it is hot.

This land, drowned in the rains of a hundred years, swells and bursts out in heavy foliage under the sudden heat; everywhere shrubs, grasses, the merest brushwood, all push out green branches such as we have never seen. It is the very finest weather; our island is a garden of tulips and roses, a garden of eternal flowers.

I have found my friend again, early in the morning, on the west coast; he appears anxious, uncomfortable, as if the fine weather did not suit him. I, on the contrary, am feeling very happy without knowing why; only no doubt because of the weather. The road gives off the scent of fennel; the day looks as if it will be even more wonderful than the preceding ones.

When I questioned Malus, I thought I understood from his indistinct replies that he was ill, but he did not say from what he was suffering, and his step was as lively as usual, and then I thought too that it was one of his mood swings, to which I have by now become accustomed.

We walk along the seashore, thinking of nothing; at least not I myself, happy to just feel the sun on my body. The swallows from the sea chase each other in circles on the beach up to the edge of the sea, jumping in front of the waves, then chasing after them and arguing with loud cries over some prey that is quickly swallowed.

We are just leaving the coast for a while in order to rejoin the next indentation which a shoulder of the dune hides from us, when all of a sudden my companion stops, listening… We can hear only the sea on all sides, the tranquil sea, regular and even, not wild and tempestuous as during the periods of the equinox.

I am preparing to continue our walk when an arm seizes me in desperation. "Don't go any farther!" Malus says to me in a different voice, that of a child who is afraid of the dark. Astonished, I ask him why: the seashore ahead of us, which I know well, is quite small, well sheltered, agreeable in every way, furnished with a few large rocks from which we can contemplate the waves, one after another, at our ease.

"Don't go any farther," he says again vehemently, "there is nothing for you on this beach."

"Well then," I say, amused, "not anywhere else either."

"For the love of God, do not go on! Yesterday's tide brought the devils of summer up onto the sand, the terrifying human fish that have come down from the hot seas and are only here to seek our death."

"What stories are you telling me now?"

"The sirens! The sirens have descended on our unfortunate island!"

"Are you mad? We know perfectly well that the sirens do not exist."

"Don't go on! They only know how to mock you. The boat that is waiting for us will come from the other side…"

But I am already not listening any more; I can only hear the song that rises from the sea, nostalgic and at the same time joyous, from whence I suddenly hear my name called.

Feebly the voice of my friend calls me back: "Come back, come back, you have no idea…" With a few bounds, I am on top of the verge.

The young women are bronzing their mother-of-pearl skin in the sun after their bath, wearing only necklaces and bracelets of seashells. At first I am afraid that they will flee at my approach, and how then can I make a gesture to show my admiration towards them… The sand begins slowly running through my empty head.

I perceive the one who is waiting for me, sitting apart; she is watching me contemplatively; from her half-raised right hand the sand is falling, piling up behind my forehead and my eyes with a barely perceptible rustling. I let myself slide to the bottom of the crumbling dune.

"How long you have been," she says. "Look at all the days that I have been following the traces of your steps on the beach and for a long time now I have adorned myself, thinking of you; I would let my body undulate when I walked to please you; if I started to sing, your name would come endlessly to my mouth in spite of myself, and when swimming I could feel the caress of your hands running over my arms."

I take her long hand, her harpist's hand; one by one I count her nimble fingers. Her skin is so soft and polished by the waves that one has to tremble on touching it. Her hand is so white and her fingers are so slender that the ring I picked up slides onto her third finger without difficulty.

The bay, now incredibly deserted, stretches out at our feet; the sea has pulled back its fish and seaweed, so far this time that they will never return: the rocks have closed the passage behind them. The sea has left for ever for colder shores.

"Who are you, you sad man, man with the grey eyes and lonely face who frightens me so much? From what distant time have I not been allowed to hope that you would not flee from me before the ice that you bring? Wisps of the mist are still caught in your wool; the lips on your mouth are too thin and hardly ever speak, your large open eyes see no farther than their eyelids, your ears are pricked up but they hear nothing.

"But all the same my head has already left a mark in the hollow of your shoulder, these eyes reflect the image of my own and these calloused palms easily hold the shape of my thighs…"

He broadened his smile as he looked at the beautiful girl who was watching him, with kindness it seemed to him. Then the traffic policeman blew his whistle and the line of cars that had stopped at the crossing continued up the avenue. The young girl, before driving out of sight at the wheel of her car, gave him a slight nod of her head.

At that moment he had the impression of having already met her, but he couldn't think where it was nor when. Or had he perhaps only been smiling at a stranger? It was certainly not impossible after all: it did not cost her anything `to catch his attention like that, and she would probably never see him again. Even if he were to see her again, would he recognize her? It was not very likely; and then perhaps she did not even live in the capital, she might even be a foreigner. He should have looked at her licence plate; now it was too late. He buried himself again in his newspaper.

Boris, sitting on a bench, was taking advantage of the late September sun. She had not been to the factory for two days, the weather was fine, and so he passed most of the afternoon on the town benches, sometimes in the public gardens, or else on the terraces of the cafés.

He read the newspapers haphazardly, but with a definite preference for any news that concerned the King, noticing a certain annoyance in himself that the latter were so numerous and so devoid of the strict and ceremonial character that one had a right to expect. It was quite certain that the press had recently been giving more attention to the smallest and most intimate details of his daily life, which now stretched out across their columns, and which had the effect of giving him a kind of human warmth, which was even more evident now that Boris, on the contrary, planned to destroy him.

This situation could not continue. It had been particularly shocking that Wednesday morning that the papers took no account of the assassination of the day before, only carried out in his imagination admittedly, but still of much more consequence than the thousand trivial items that they reported with such banality. Perhaps he would have to bribe an editor. It was very humiliating to have to resort to such methods.

Would he not have done better to have left some indication of his passage, "the weapon left at the scene of the crime" as a provocation, to overcome this indifference? On the other hand it was important to keep the knife as a proof in case there were any doubts. Indeed it was childish to get upset over so little: he had not killed the King, it was only the seventeenth of September and the visit was planned for the eighteenth. The reasonable course of action was to be patient until then; the matter had been well planned, well put together, well organized, and would certainly attract attention when the time came.

The vertical-assembly plant had been built expressly with this murder in mind: the disposition of the rooms, the functioning of the lift, the lock on the little door, all had been ordered for this single purpose, and because of this the project had to succeed. The King himself was coming with the intention of ending his days, considering no doubt that he was an obstacle in the march of history: as he could not abdicate without creating problems, he would prefer this kind of suicide. Everything would come about as if he himself had stopped the lift at the unused platform in order to plunge the knife into his heart and then to offer it, red with his blood, to Boris, his only friend, his sole kinsman, as a token of his affection.

It was therefore a talisman, and all that had to be done was to present it at the palace in order to be installed, furnished with this sceptre, on the throne of the dead man; because it would be him, Boris, that the collective will would choose to be King, while handing over the General Factory to his pleasure, and later on in prompting to him every word of his new role.

He let his eyes wander over the crowd of his subjects who were passing around him. The advance signs of his new dignity began to shine out amid the general indifference: hundreds of eyes were fixed on him, the most beautiful of his vassals had just smiled at him through the lowered window of her car.

Something had to be done for this waiting populace. The rapid rise of the Church was perhaps an unfavourable event for the state; King John was debonair, but Boris, while remaining fully responsible, must first of all clearly examine the reasons for the problems which weighed down the state on every side. There was still time to change direction: the masses, pressured by the party agitation, seemed to be hesitant, but could be persuaded to rise without difficulty against those who had provoked them.

The Unionist programme seemed to be tempting enough with its projects for new constructions: the new roads that would stretch out to all parts of the country, of which enormous areas were still unexplored, even unknown. And then there was the Church with its parades and its cathedrals. How to decide what to do? Flip a coin? Heads or tails?

Heads.

Right at the end of the immense beach left dry by the tide, we come to the little cloudy lagoon that constitutes the last leftovers of the ocean.

Aimone, in order to rest, lets herself slide into the warm water and stretches out on the sandy bottom among the sea grasses, thanks to this strange gift that women have here to breathe in the sea. With her eyes open, her lips loose, her long flowing hair undulating around her body, she looks at me through the dull blue-green water which half-veils her; I lean over, seeking out her limbs between the green creepers. She smiles, reaches out a hand to the surface as if to pull me towards her. But to what purpose? She well knows that I cannot live without air and I begin to curse this water which separates us. One would say that she is speaking, although no sound comes to my ears and, suddenly taken by panic, I seize this arm which calls to me, and I pull it to me towards the surface; when finally her face emerges, I lie down in turn next to her and caress her, Aimone, gentle stray piece of flotsam among all the floating seaweed. Dissolved in the lukewarm liquid we love each other, both of us half drowned...

Soon the sea has thrown us up on the beach where we lie stretched out, dreaming like dead bodies after drowning; and slowly, with regret, the memory returns.

She has the same long, supple body, still childlike almost; her bronzed skin shone just as much under the green water and she had the slightly bitter taste of kelp.

She was called Lelia... Lelia with the fragile eyes, with her distant soul and soft flesh. Lelia with ash-blond hair which fell back over her shoulders and whose graceful limbs enabled her easily to outswim me. Lelia, tea rose, where are you now? Why did you not come back to me all the same, you whom I never tried to hold and whose return I never expected, Lelia for whom I never cried, and who without any doubt never cried for me either, insouciant and always cheerful; what have I to do today with your seductive image?

I look at Aimone, little dislocated brittle star; it is indeed she, as one lamb resembles another.

"Last summer," she says, "you had a paler colour and your muscles were less developed."

"It's because I have been rowing in the wind and the rain, but I don't understand what you are saying: are we not seeing each other for the first time?"

"Of course," she replies, as if coming out of a dream, "I was talking of someone else."

10

THAT SUMMER IT WAS REALLY VERY HOT; it was not that suffocating heat that prostrates the body and makes it feel ill, but a benevolent collapse in the generalized torpor, a kind of abyss that sucked everything into itself. It was certainly too hot to be working, too hot as well to take long walks; Boris had been forced to give up his interminable hikes over the bogs and the plains, and in any case he no longer felt the need; he spent whole days and nights lying on the sand next to Aimone, capturing the slight breath of air that came from the sea, which saved them from too heavy a stupor.

The most torrid hours were passed in the healing water; without moving they let themselves be carried, barely conscious, like translucent jellyfish, softened, soaked, their consciousness dissolved.

On the beaches the dried seaweed had been bleached white by the baking sun; the overheated dunes recovered their look of dead vegetation. In the centre of the island, after the luxuriance of the early sun, the pretty colours quickly changed to a yellowish grey: it was similar to the colour of winter, albeit dustier. Only the swamps still retained an appearance of freshness: there, the persistent humidity had given birth to a real tropical flowering, which from day to day grew to ever more unexpected dimensions.

The harvest of rye and barley had been more abundant than we had ever seen before, the spears having barely had time to ripen before they were grilled by the heat of the August sun. Along the low walls of dry stone the brambles had intertwined their large berries, black and perfumed, with the violet stars of the bittersweet nightshade; and in the little gardens, near the village, we had gathered some fine pears.

But the drought had very quickly brought its ravages. We had to dig up, well before their time, the late potatoes, which had stopped growing; in the scorched pastures the sheep could no longer find a blade of grass. We had hastily built shelters of branches to protect the animals, and they would come to them from the early morning, seeking shade; it was there that we brought them a little straw and a few buckets of precious water which soon threatened to run out.

Malus had disappeared and everyone had forgotten him; the young men were living with the sirens and thought no more of the slightly bent silhouette which used to make them feel uneasy in the fog. Some of them, having wandered as far as the tip of the northern coast, would say that he was hiding behind the thick walls of his tower. Locked in the most obscure room, in which he had blocked off the only loophole, with every exit sealed off, he had managed to protect himself from the heat and the blinding light.

Outside the walls the sun invaded everything, numbing even the lizards and making even the fish fall into a stupor, which no one had the strength to gather in. The old people in the village were saying that such weather must soon end.

Boris sat down on a box; he was feeling a great tiredness throughout his body and particularly in his legs, which were shaking and unsure of themselves. His head felt even heavier than on most days.

Naturally he had come far too early. According to the plan that he had prepared a long time ago, he would arrive just at the last moment in order to reduce the risk of discovery as much as possible; someone might open the little door unexpectedly in order to leave another packet of metal rods among the pile of waste objects and miscellaneous materials. How could Boris explain his presence in this obscure place?

The best would be to look busy, as if he had just brought something there, or as if he were looking for a tool that had supposedly been left there. But the other person might be a foreman, a technician of some kind sent to verify a technical detail or even to inspect the perimeter of the royal route; he would immediately see that Boris did not belong there. Even given the most favourable circumstances, with no person interrupting him, it was stupid to be there for hours with his nerves on edge... No, it wasn't that, he was not nervous: he was more afraid of falling asleep.

Everything was exactly as he remembered it, except that the platform seemed to be less in darkness: a bluish light was shining over the whole area instead of emanating only from the lift cage. Boris was asking himself if he would have to put the light on, when he suddenly remembered that the last time the light had suddenly gone on as soon as he had pressed the stop button; and he was fairly certain that he had not pressed the other button at the same time, so it would be just as useless to do it today; perhaps after all the second button had nothing to do with the lighting as he had thought, and the first one had two uses at the same time; it might well be an alarm bell that he must at all costs avoid setting off.

Yet a separate functioning must have been foreseen, and so it would be normal to have a lift button that also turned on the light, and another one for the light alone. Something always went wrong: it was not rational to press the second button if doing so served no purpose, but to do so after realizing that the light would not go on – which was always possible after all – was at the same time a delay and a disruption to his plan. The uncertainty was even more irritating because Boris did not know exactly what its origin was, as no attempt had yet been made "in reality".

He tried to settle down more comfortably on his box, looking into the dimness to see if there was not a better seat. He had to make do with leaning his back against a small beam after making sure that it was reasonably clean: he had to be careful not to get his clothes dirty, as well as not leaving marks in the dust.

His suit had in any case given him some problems: he could hardly turn up at the gates of the factory in work overalls; on the other hand, carrying such a garment in under his arm hoping to find a quiet corner would complicate matters. After many hesitations, he had come dressed in an ordinary suit, neither too worn nor too new, and it was only when he came into the main lobby that he had realized his mistake; in the crowd, not very dense at this time, there were only two categories of person: workers in blue overalls who were finalizing the preparations and others dressed in their best who had come to rehearse their part in the ceremony. At the time, everything had seemed to him to be lost, but then, observing that everyone was too busy to notice him, he had decided to proceed as if everything was going according to plan.

He had then started to climb the staircase, concentrating on the actions that he was going to accomplish. But as he climbed, he felt, on the contrary, his confidence escaping him; he could not succeed in persuading himself that this time he was really going to commit a crime. From minute to minute a void grew in his head. He should have drunk a sleeping draught the night before to be sure of sleeping properly, on that night at least; on the other hand that might have increased this sluggishness from which he was suffering just when he needed all his wits about him. It would have been better to have taken a sleeping draught for several nights and then a stimulant on the morning in question; but it wasn't as easy as all that and above all it was unnatural: nothing good could come from using all these drugs.

As things stood, he must behave like a robot carrying out an action that it has learnt by rote; he was not fully in control, not more than he would have been had he opted for the previous solution. What's more, if an unexpected happening disrupted him in the act, he would commit the worst mistakes at random; but as an *unexpected* happening would indicate an error in his preparations, even if he were able to turn it to his advantage at the decisive moment, the carrying out of the act would still be entirely compromised. So there was no question of putting off the enterprise to later on: if it was necessary to do it, it would succeed now.

After the first landing, he had come across two men dressed like himself; initially this had pleased him, but he had no sooner passed them than he found their appearance sloppy; he had turned round to inspect them once again and he saw the two men, who had also turned around, looking at him. Extremely worried, he went on his way; it was as if he had received a blow to the head.

Luckily, he did not know them, because if he had had to sustain a conversation, even if only for a few seconds, he would have seemed like a madman.

On reflection, Boris thought that perhaps he had met his colleagues after all, and that he had passed them without recognizing them, which was even more awkward.

It was too hot in this storeroom and it was difficult to breathe. Boris was tempted to leave. All the same he wanted to finish matters once and for all: tacking things up on the wall and other surrogates was not good enough, what was needed was a gesture that really committed the body of its instigator.

Why become discouraged? The affair was going well; there had been no serious mishap until now: the stairway, the security control, the little corridor and the door... Sitting on his box, Boris saw again the little man with the cunning smile; the King was laughing at him.

Why does my friend not come to visit me any more? It's a long time since I heard from him: two months, three months? It is impossible to make the most simple calculation under this sun, nor to remember anything precisely. What did he say to me during our walks? Perhaps he made promises and, as he is unable to keep them, he is avoiding my questions; or perhaps he is afraid of the heat? Aside from that, everything has worked out for the best: the staircase, the security control, the little corridor, the door... and the days go on, calm without expectations, nothing ahead of them, nothing behind, but leisure and somnolence.

We inhabit those zones which are seldom explored, where the sand is a bit like clay, where monstrous shellfish bristling with sharp points are everywhere, interlocking pincers and claws, voracious mouths without body; in the pools around us flaccid creatures dissolve, slightly revolting, which change their shape the minute you take them out of the water...

At the moment that he had turned round to escape the look of the two men, he found himself nose to nose with a group of uniformed guards who were conducting a security check on the second landing. He was already on the point of going down again when he realized that such a course of action would make him suspect; so he gave his straightest face as he showed his pass, which testified that he was employed in the factory, pretending to believe that this simple card was enough to justify his presence in this place. At the same time he noticed, beside him, an individual who went straight through the barrier without stopping while exhibiting a similar card; he understood immediately that that was all one had to do and regretted that he had not gone straight through like all the others, casually, without waiting to have it explained that the passage was free. And then too, in order to account for the slight hesitation which had got him noticed, he had asked one of the guards for the time, but he had been so worried that he had not registered the reply.

The more he thought about it, the more he found the security check unbelievable: it would have been normal to have at least looked at the number of the workshop, because tens of thousands of workers carried a card of the General Factory, and it was even probable that anyone could obtain one without much difficulty. Perhaps employees coming from different departments had reason for coming here on an exceptional day; in that case any verification was illusory, there should at least be a special pass for the circumstances. Anyhow, the current pass was already asked for by the door-man at the big gate and no one could come in without one.

This travesty could only have the purpose of keeping up appearances: all precautions seemed to be superfluous, and artificial measures were being taken for the sake of form.

Boris stood up to exercise his legs a little but, afraid of making a conspicuous noise, he did not dare take the few steps that would have relieved his cramp. He looked at his watch: it had stopped again; he thought of opening the box, but unfortunately the light was not good enough. He sat down again, the box creaking feebly.

All of a sudden he remembered that he had not even worked out his movements; where was his head after all? He rose again, pleased to have a pretext to move. The buttons were there all right: the three big ones for the lift, up, down, stop – one could just read the three words – and the little one above it, which could only be for the light. All the same, Boris would have liked to be certain, but he was afraid of raising an alarm. He tried to imagine what other mechanism there could be, but could not come up with anything: it had to be the light. And then perhaps it was not working? That on its own would not be important, the half-light was good enough. So why bother to turn it on?

In order to think of something else, he fingered the knife in his pocket, then went to sit down again while he made himself mentally go over, one more time, the motions he was going to carry out, instead of endlessly digesting the reasons that had brought him here. He only managed to carry out unproductive work, which threatened to bog him down in fixed ideas, which were dangerous on that account. He was running idle: as soon as he heard the click of the lift beginning to move he would wait at his post, seizing the knife hidden in his pocket... Mechanically he made the gesture;

a little wave had just worked up to his feet, he pulled back a little on the sand.

Having a little trouble opening the lock on entering, he had not dared to close it in case he found himself caught in a trap; it was a nuisance: someone might worry at seeing the little door open. He unrolled the piece of paper and folded it carefully... another wave, stronger this time, one might say that the water was beginning to rise.

He turned his eyes towards Aimone, who was sleeping underneath his hand in an abandoned pose, a starfish forgotten on the beach, helpless, at his mercy. A stronger wave rolled over her body; she sat up suddenly, shivering, and said, "It's cold!" Boris got up as well.

Then he asked himself what he was doing standing up, again he felt the knife in his pocket and sat down again on the box.

As soon as he could hear the click, he would go to his post... What time could it be now? It was difficult to breathe in this tunnel, everywhere there was a disagreeable odour of acetylene. Perhaps it was toxic; Boris saw the royal cabin slowly rising towards the platform, lighting his own corpse on the way up.

Naturally the water was warm as usual; Aimone, who had been drowsy, had certainly been surprised by its sudden touch.

All the same, at that hour of the day, a relative coolness can be felt; above all today, because a good breeze had been blowing since the morning.

To talk of "warming up" seemed to be absurd all the same. What strange nature does this girl have? I have lazily followed her in her activities; far from satisfying her, she now wants us to go "somewhere else". Where does she think we can go?

"Come," she says to me, "it will be cold tonight." But she does not insist so much that I should go with her; when I try to seize her she escapes me and, penetrating the water with a leap, she distances herself with rapid strokes. She cries out to me again: "I will return!" Then I hear her laugh, which leaves me undecided as to what I should think.

It is pleasant on this beach; in the softness of the twilight, and without questioning myself any further, I watch Aimone swimming in the waves...

Boris jumped up: the cabin was rising! Having bounded from his seat, he suddenly thought that he had forgotten the knife; seized with fear, he searched the inside pocket of his jacket; obviously the knife was there, as he had already verified many times. Then all emotion suddenly stopped and he started to go through his sequence of mechanical movements.

The cabin was rising with a low regular humming. Boris looked at the narrow blade; the King would perhaps be wearing a hidden bulletproof vest. The "fatal moment" was at hand.

He noticed at once that neither the King, nor anyone else, was in the lift; his immediate instinct was to throw himself backward, but he contained himself: what did he have to fear from this empty cabin? All the same, he was only a little surprised. He waited. The metal cage came to a stop just at the platform, and almost immediately started to go down again.

What did this palaver mean? A test, or perhaps a demonstration? The right time must have passed some time ago. He stayed all the same, but he did not really believe what was happening.

Once again the cabin was on the ground floor, the sound of the motor had stopped. Boris wondered whether to sit down again; but the thought didn't appeal very much. He watched the tiny head that was disappearing slowly into the sea; one could no longer tell if it was a head at this distance, in the twilight; it could just as easily be a seagull resting on the water.

Boris was breathing in the smell of the rising tide when the irritating noise of the motor aroused him. He continued nevertheless to clutch at the blonde hair each time that she appeared, but she became more and more confused with the froth on the crest of the waves. Where was she going like this in the falling night? A wave splattered his legs; he stepped back.

There was nothing more to be seen, Boris climbed up to sit down on a dune. There were two people now in front of him: why not two after all? One was standing a little to one side, it was not a particular nuisance.

The sea shone faintly in the light of the stars; the moon had not yet risen.

11

S UDDENLY EVERYTHING became a muddle.

The King had already started to move forward, thinking he had arrived at his destination and not showing surprise at being received in this dusty storeroom... He had had, at the moment that Boris struck him, an incredulous look, distinguished by a slightly ironic frown at the unlikeliness of the attack; but at the same instant – immediately afterwards or a few seconds before? – pistol shots rang out, coming, so it seemed, a bit from everywhere, from behind the boxes which were piled up on the platform. Boris had succeeded, not without difficulty, in withdrawing his knife and, in a frenzy, had sent the lift down again. During this time, to heighten the disorder, a bell had gone off, while shouts were rebounding from everywhere.

There was nothing to do now but get away, but the alarm bells were sounding and multiplying through all the stairways and corridors; Boris ran as fast as he could through an uncontrolled fracas of whistles and bells. As he ran, two rows of frightened faces looked at him in terror. Throwing a look at his hands, he saw that they were covered in blood and he ran faster.

He no longer knew where he was; only one thing occupied his mind: who had fired, what kind of people were they? Conspirators, hidden like himself, or police? For criminals waiting in ambush they had remained very quiet and seemed to rely entirely on him to stop the cabin; it's true that they could have foreseen another mechanism to make it come up, and perhaps the lift had stopped when he himself had pressed the button. In any case, the weapons they had chosen allowed them to act without stopping the lift, which only moved slowly; but it seemed strange, if that was their intention, that they had not fired earlier. On the other hand, if one supposed that they were policemen, it was equally incomprehensible that they had waited so long and behaved afterwards with such inefficiency. Had they arrived on the scene too late?

None of this was clear to Boris, who could not even remember *when* the fusillade had begun. One image assailed him: that of two policemen leaning over his body riddled with bullets; in the cabin, which had resumed its upward path, the King was tidying the disorder of his outfit, while the man who accompanied him was excusing himself for not having intervened with more presence of mind: "It all happened so quickly," he was saying; but the King was amiably reassuring him: "It's nothing, these madmen are never very dangerous."

Boris was still running between the astonished groups of people. Unable to wait any longer, as he passed a pillar which put him out of sight of the curious bystanders, he took the kitchen knife out of his pocket that he had forgotten to roll again in its paper: there was definitely blood on the blade, that at least was not an illusion. He smiled with a satisfied air – "After all," he said to himself, "there is some proof," and he walked on more calmly.

All the same, many other details worried him; there had been a second person in the lift, whose behaviour was not clear: why had he not moved during all that was happening? Had he been shot dead at the beginning by a revolver shot, his body still standing up, leaning against the partition? Or had he acted in some way, unbeknownst to Boris? Perhaps he was the one who had called for help and set off the alarm signal; or else perhaps it had been Boris himself by some accidental manoeuvre. Which exactly were the buttons he had pressed in his stupor and haste? He could not even say exactly at what precise moment the bell had gone off: in a general way the chronology of the matter escaped him totally.

His last hope of understanding all this was to read, with a clear head, the explanations which the papers would not fail to publish the next day. Until then every interpretation was possible, for example that the King had first of all been killed by the others and that his own role had consisted only of drawing attention to the murder.

Later on I thought that she would not come back that evening, or even that she would not come back at all; it was not at all the same to me, but there was no hurry. It was a little less hot, and I buttoned up the collar of my shirt.

I stayed there a little longer, without moving, looking at my half-closed hands through which the sand from the sea had just been running; all that remained was this uncertain trace: a brilliant dust of mother of pearl and mica sticking a little here and there, but soon detaching itself from my too dry fingers, leaving them irreversibly whole, at the end of my dangling arms.

The night must have been already well advanced. The sea had reached the last line of seaweed at the top of the beach; after the billows of the day, appeased now, it has become silent.

By the path through the dune, I walked along the narrow border that the high tide was now abandoning; at the limit of the water, drenched by a wave a little stronger than the others, a strip of gravel shone softly under the clear sky.

The wind had fallen and left the long strands of sharp grass immobile and hard to see on the ground in the darkness.

I had walked straight in front of me for hours, my limbs weary, my head empty, and I was no more than this fringe of shining stones which bordered the water line. At times the path, moving in a little towards the plain, robbed me of their feeble shine; then I walked out of control, like someone going down the stairs of a lighthouse who suddenly realizes that he has lost the handrail and staggers, incapable of remembering the way down vividly enough.

My head was even emptier than the large shells which keep the sound of the waves always present; I was nothing more than this emptiness, and even the ocean itself and all the sands of its beaches could not suffice to fill it.

With dawn the shore could be seen again, large and flat, where the receding tide had left visible tufts of bladderwrack exposed; lower down the brown tresses were bathed in an undertow of discoloured water with the slow rocking that follows love. A light odour of iodine floated on the rising wind.

I lie down to rest, my back against a rock, on which my diligent hands, these hands that cannot retain the shape of gestures they have made nor of things they have touched, recognize their brother, the granite, that time has not been able to make smooth. And then a little song has come to my lips in the strident morning pierced with the cries of the swallows; I was still alive.

The village seemed farther away than I ever would have believed, and I forced my pace to get there faster, because I was in a hurry to eat a piece of bread and go to sleep. Arriving at the big bay, I saw the houses shining in the rising sun in front of me; I recognized my own, a little apart, and it gave me pleasure.

On the side of the land, a trace of fog blocked the view. It was almost cold at this moment; I was happy to be back.

From six o'clock in the evening until eight in the morning, Boris slept like a log. He woke up, his spirits doleful but at rest. Getting out of bed without any particular intention of doing anything at all, he wandered around his room in his pyjamas, from the window to the bedside table; having reached the washbasin almost by chance, he made some attempt at his toilet. But all that did not succeed in putting him at ease. He looked at the little canvas on the wall and smiled at it indulgently. He was swimming.

When he turned round, he saw the portrait of the late King and gave him a sign of connivance; the crumpled face returned his salute. Boris neatly took out the drawing pins, carefully tore up the picture, put the pieces into the ashtray and went back to bed.

He had no appetite to go out to eat; he felt fine where he was, doing nothing. A grey band had appeared in the west, just above the horizon, he looked towards the north, where the sky remained irreproachably blue and said: "It's just as fine as it was, just as fine as it can be." Aimone, who was floating beside him, made no reply.

There was a regular knocking just underneath his room, loud enough to shake the partition wall; it was irritating in the middle of this calm. Boris got out of bed, and the knocks ceased almost immediately. As he was up he looked for something to do, went towards the photograph of the King hanging on the wall and, having taken it down, tore it up calmly. Then he slid back between the sheets.

Today too there was a little swell which made his body rock, and made him nauseous in the end. He took out of the drawer the knife which at other times he used to peel vegetables; the spots on the blade had dried and were surrounded by a border of rust, it was not clear what it was; however, on the paper in which it was wrapped there were traces left by a red liquid. Everything was going well: the King was dead.

In a moment Boris would get up to buy a newspaper and to read the account of the assassination: "Odious Crime, Act of Folly, National Mourning." Apart from a few lines insinuating that the regicide must have been politically motivated – paid from abroad – the press opinion was unanimous: it was the work of a lunatic; the weapon that had been employed, the light that the assassin had used, the cries that he had uttered, etc. What other reason, after all, could there be that could have led him brutally to sacrifice such a good sovereign who had led his people with so much wisdom, intelligence, etc., etc. And everywhere there were laudatory biographies of the deceased, accounts of his service and his intimate life; never had one been able to learn so much before.

It was upsetting in the end: this good King was now dead, so let's not talk about it any more!

During the course of the week which had now ended, the progress made by the Church had been so considerable that all serious opposition seemed to have been almost wiped out; it all happened as if by magic: the other parties, whose weakness was now obvious, were in total disintegration, their few members racing to swell the ranks of the winner; their leaders had fallen into step.

In every social stratum, the propaganda was bearing fruit; the parade that Boris had thought of as vulgar had succeeded at any event in mobilizing the so-called passive masses into a veritable political fever; everyone wanted to take part, in their enthusiasm, in the "immense task of recovery".

But in the meantime the foundations of this recovery had not yet been made clear. Certainly the building of new public installations, combined with the restoration of old ones, would easily provide work for everyone. Trains overflowing with singing workers were leaving the capital, sent off with flags, flowers and music; enormous work camps were waiting for them, so it was said, in the provinces, where innumerable building sites were going up daily. Right from the beginning unemployment had come to an end, even workers with jobs had given them up to take part in this crusade, so much so that there was now a shortage of workers everywhere.

But no one could see where all this was leading. What could all these constructions bring back to the state? They were already costing it an enormous amount and, if taken to the extent that was planned, they would use up the greater part of the national budget. The faithful were plentiful, but all the religious ceremonies had until now been free for those attending them, and one should not count too much on foreign tourists to defray the expenses of the state. In brief, there was no way that the cathedrals could be seen to provide future riches.

On the other hand the external situation was still very alarming. Everyone had embarked on this unreasonable euphoria as if they were counting on the epidemic to calm the appetite of their neighbours and just as firmly on their faith to stabilize the financial situation.

This confidence in things irritated Boris: when he had asked Laura what this "politics" really meant, all she could answer was that once people were properly warmed up, they could accomplish great things. But he wanted first to know the truth of the matter: if the plans of the Church had to be kept secret, then it must be because they would be unacceptable in the cold light of day. Laura claimed that the most important thing was to waken the national conscience: was it not, voluntarily or not, continually being put to sleep? Boris, on the other hand, could not prevent himself from thinking that there was no purpose behind all this activity, that all the noise was only an end in itself, and to such an extent that all this work produced nothing at all; that was what horrified him most.

Laura radiated certainty and that was what was equally insufferable. New elections, which were now necessary, would confirm next month that the entire people... Boris would not have been unhappy if his little crime were to bring all these little platitudes to an end. The late King had in fact revealed himself as one of the party's trump cards, the leaders of which, forming a more or less secret committee, having need of a standard bearer; they had found in him a person who was both convenient and little trouble: the heir to a tradition, the sovereign could in no way support any dangerous revolutionary ideas, and, in any case, incarnating the very principle of order, how could he cause them the slightest problem? In their capable hands he had become popular in a few days, whereas he could just as easily have been forgotten altogether. In addition, he had always practised his religion, which had facilitated the sleight of hand: there was really only one party, and the most amiable of kings was its chief.

But then, just at this moment, this King died by assassination. If there had been any real opponents, the Church would have been able to take advantage of the situation to exterminate them for being responsible, they would also have used the pretext of the murder to start a war of conquest, but they had no opposition and it seemed only too evident that the country was not ready for a war which, even with a large army of fanatics, could only bring about disaster. It was difficult to see how this regicide could help them, even considering that the young prince would be even easier to influence.

On the other hand it was always possible that King John had been the real head of the Church, and that it was on that account that he had lost his head.

On the floor below, the pounding had started again, even louder. Boris lent his ear in order to find out what was happening. "They must be building a cathedral," he joked to himself. "Can there be any other activity in the world?"

The noise stopped. Boris did not divert his attention, expecting it to start again and doubting at the same time that it would. The radio was speaking in a neutral tone and he distinctly heard: "…the end of the speech given yesterday by His Highness King John at the end of the ceremony which took place at the General Factory", and immediately afterwards the little voice, benevolent and mischievous. The King was still in good health.

The banging started up again. This time it sounded as if it was not going to stop for a long time. Boris rose, he was feeling tired, his limbs were even heavier than his head; all the same he started to dress. From the wall the photograph smiled into its little beard. He murmured: "I've been wasting my time," then he went out to eat something.

In the café at the next table, someone was reading a newspaper; at the sight of the printed pages he felt a strange sensation in his stomach. The waiter looked at him from far away; instead of coming to take his order, he switched on the radio and turned the buttons: the little voice continued talking into its beard...

The speech was interminable. The surge having become stronger, he would have liked to be swimming more vigorously in order to reach the beach as quickly as possible, but he was exhausted; he could see Aimone under the green water, lying on the sand a few metres below him, watching him calmly. There were no waves down there where she was. In the middle of the plaudits of the crowd, the factory band struck up a hymn by way of national anthem; the sea took on the deep cadence of the music.

The visit was a success. It was the turn of the minister of public works to talk; the member of the Church, if ever there was one, skilfully mingled points of propaganda with flattery of the workers: unity, pride in our work and in the greatness of the country; law, faith, king, joy, you, me, no sitting on the fence; it was an electoral speech. Boris paid the bill and left; in his head there was a hourglass which was running out regularly; when all the sand had passed through the centre from top to bottom, it had to be turned over, that is to say one had to walk on one's hands; no doubt that would be difficult, but he could see no other solution.

Fortunately the flood was slowing down; his head, which at the moment was in the upper part of the glass, was half-blocking the passage, it was too big to pass through and was preventing the sand from flowing. Being now very near the beach, he found his feet and came out of the water; his exhaustion was total, he had difficulty in dragging himself back to his room.

Once there, he found himself again looking at the smiling face in the portrait; the drawing pin in the left-hand lower corner was not in the right place; it had slipped in an annoying way towards the middle of the picture; he removed it to replace it exactly in its corner. In the drawer of the bedside table he found a knife, unwrapped it from its paper, soiled by unclean traces not easy to identify. With a match he lit the paper and watched it in the mirror as it burned in front of his own face. Then he started to clean the blade, scratching it with the help of his nail file.

The flame having entirely consumed the strip of paper, there was nothing more to be seen in the mirror than the greenish depths which are not water as I had at first thought, but the half-light of an undergrowth.

During the course of the summer all kinds of new vegetation had appeared, of which the foliage noticeably changed the landscape; it was in the middle of the island that the change was especially jarring: what until now had been stunted shrubs took on the appearance and the dimensions of real trees, and there was no modest herbaceous plant that did not in its sudden proliferation reach the height of a man, so much so that we had considerable difficulty among all this growth to find the old paths.

At that moment I was strolling through a narrow clearing in a wood, treading down the tall grass, dried by the sun of the previous months, with my feet; I was walking along happily (because the overcast sky made it possible once again), thinking I was following an old pathway, but my passage progressively narrowed into a forest path which seems to me so different from what I was expecting that I struggle to recognize it: besides its unusual appearance, the direction in which it leads does not appear promising.

I want to get to the little beach before nightfall: I have taken this route to get there faster, and now I fear at every moment that I have made a mistake. In some places the path completely disappears under the tangled brambles that catch my clothes and tear them when I pull away too sharply; farther on it becomes visible again, only to lose itself once more among the pine trees. I must have strayed too far to the right, because I find the path again a few metres to the side, this time much more recognizable, hardly covered by the grass; a doubt remains with me as to its direction, but at the same time I think I remember this flat stone, shaped like a tombstone which rises a little above the ground; I had once amused myself by deciphering the characters written on it.

But later on the scrub had thickened to such an extent that I had to give up any idea of getting through it: it was not possible that such a passage went through there, because I can see ahead of me trees that could not have grown in a single season, even with this heat. I retrace my steps and discover, a few hundred metres higher up, a fork so wide that I am amazed not to have noticed it earlier. Unfortunately it is not long before it too abandons me.

Several times I change direction in this way, I turn around, I move off on a new path, but more and more I feel that I am lost; whenever a clearing allows me to take a few steps forward, it is only to lead me the more surely into the heart of the most inextricable brambles. And all the same, I had adventured that way to gain time; Aimone must be on the little sandbank; only yesterday she had complained of cold and I am afraid that she will leave without waiting for me. Or else, seeing the heavy sky, would she have renounced coming at all?

Something resembling a path branches off to the left, but where does it lead? If it is not where I want to go, the faster I push ahead the farther I am distancing myself from my goal; on the other hand, wherever it leads, the more I slow down, the less chance I have of ever arriving anywhere at all. As I have no idea at all where I am, it is quite possible that the path is the right one, but that I should take it in the other direction.

In the middle of these thoughts I find myself again in front of the tombstone: clearly I am turning in circles. After having walked farther, haphazardly, into a tangle, more and more caught up in the branches which scratch my face and the tree trunks which block my passage, I stop, abandoning my struggle. I had thought that I would make it through this traverse unscathed. The forest, it seems, has closed in on me.

12

THE FISHING SEASON IS OVER; our boats, already pulled up onto the ground, are waiting to be put into shelter until next year. Today Guilhem and Guiraut made a short excursion, but they did not bring back any fish; nobody will go out to sea tomorrow.

A small, persistent light rain has been falling since yesterday, which seems to be trying to make up for the last few months; but it does not fall with excessive haste, it feels at home, it will take the time it needs, one week, two weeks, and soon the ditches bordering the roads will be filled again with stagnant water, and if it needs three weeks for the earth to become well and deeply impregnated, the rain, the tenacious, loyal rain, on which one can always count, will take them; it is already sure of its success, the work will be done by the book.

Then the landscape quickly returns to its normal colours, those we have known from all eternity, and which we like because they are ours. A few days more and we will no longer be able to walk through the bogs by following the built-up footways that pass through them; already this morning, when I went out to look for peat, I saw the ancient ditches more than half filled with black water, and between them the soil had become spongy again. I shall no longer dare, from now on, to stray from the paths that I recognize; sheep are often lost in the swamps and we never find any trace of them; and there are stories too of imprudent men who have certainly suffered the same fate.

It has only been raining for two days and it is as if it had never stopped raining. One by one the sirens had left with the fine weather; but who among us regrets it now that the sun has ceased to shine? It remains for us to carry out the thousand little tasks to be finished before winter comes: not big jobs certainly – there is never a big job to be done on our island – bringing in a supply of peat, protecting from the humidity as far as possible everything that risks going rotten if left outside, and carrying out the tiny repairs which are necessary for our thatched roofs, and perhaps some work in the fields before the earth becomes altogether sodden; there is nothing in all that that will kill a man, it is in a way more a distraction than real work.

It is raining, and even the aspect of this fine rain stops one from thinking that it could have a beginning and an end. It is so light that you hardly notice it; we are so accustomed to it that sometimes, carelessly, we go out without taking waterproof coverings; and then, when we come in again, we find that we are wet through to the bone in a way that we have totally forgotten about. The rain seems in fact to have become an intimate part of the air around us, we breathe it, we eat it, we drink it; we become part of a little fine rain that has no form or consistency and which makes no noise.

It is this climate which uses up our strength, it is the weather that finally causes our death. We inhabit an excessively misty island where we only see the sky for a few days a year. There is not even a real downpour, it is rather a fog – a "mizzle" we say – which saturates the atmosphere instead of falling normally; the tiny droplets weave their greyish tissue around us, the web of which is sometimes so tight that it blinds and strangles us; the wind, which is never very strong on our coasts, moves its veils around, as if arranging the folds of a shroud.

Sometimes we look for the cause of these fogs and some say that we ourselves are responsible; they blame the windmills that we have built to grind our rye, of stopping the clouds in their flight and holding them back, caught in their wooden flails, clouds that otherwise could not do otherwise but pass by; but to tell the truth it seems very improbable that such small windmills could succeed in stopping so much fog. Others think that perhaps we are wrong to retain such a large surface of swamp and that, if we could manage to dry it out at least partially, by drawing the water out to the sea, the evaporation would diminish by as much and the chance of it raining would be much less; all the same, the heat here is not so great that it can produce such strong vapours, and it would in any case be abnormal for these to be condensed so much, on the spot, instead of being blown away by the sea breezes.

The more likely explanation is that there is nothing we can do: the climate of this island is humid; the cause lies in neither our peat bogs nor our windmills, and no change can be brought about by the work we do.

We are confined to a lost world, far from any continent, stripped of port and sea wall, where no ship ever comes to call. It is not that we are surrounded by a wild sea or that dangerous currents isolate us from the main sea routes; on the contrary, these coasts are calm and safe and know few storms, even in winter, to break the serenity; and we could just as well build a jetty which would allow smaller and medium-sized vessels to float calmly in our bay, but in addition to the fact that the visibility is always too poor to remove the risk of sinking entirely, what reason could they have for coming here?

From the earliest times our ancestors have known neither invasion nor conquest: this island only produces enough to feed its little village, no stranger would want to visit it nor to subdue it.

Even though our country is not large, we do not fail when it is light to recognize its topographical features, but the plains of the south, the cliffs of the east, the dunes of the setting sun and even as far as the desert of the northern point where an abandoned tower still stands, everything is drowned in a cottony mist which makes sand and stone indistinguishable; it is often so thick that we do not dare to take a step outside; then we spend long days indoors for fear of getting lost, while all the time it pursues us into our houses; finding its way in through the tiniest crack, it fills our rooms, then our lungs, our heads, our entire bodies, which consist of nothing in the end but fog.

On one of these mornings Boris found a letter under his door, which surprised him because he never received anything at all. The irregular letters and the clumsiness of the writing gave him no clue to the identity of the sender; after having turned it over in every direction, he decided to open it after all. It was from Thomas, his office colleague, whom he had not seen since the accident.

He was recovering very slowly and seemed still to be suffering from a certain mental depression which of course prevented him from returning to his work as a statistician. He was worried and, believing that Boris was still working regularly, wanted to hear from him how things were going at the factory, asking in particular if his prolonged absence was compromising the normal flow of work. Boris was surprised by this zeal, because Thomas was generally more disposed than himself to laugh at their common duties; but now he seemed to fear that the "functioning of the department" was being "impeded" by his illness, even going so far as to write that perhaps Workshop Z, deprived of oversight, might have stopped operating. If he had known that Boris was also not going to the office, he would no doubt be worried for the economy of the whole country. He was in fact pressing his colleague to "plough through", until he was able to return, as much work as possible, if not the work of two people, which he considered difficult to achieve. He reproached himself for having so often wasted his time smoking and daydreaming or discussing futile problems; but he was now cured from that point of view: Boris, now on his own, would not let himself be put off his duty by the presence of another, which, "whatever one says, is always a nuisance".

"At least," he went on, "if they have decided to replace me temporarily, I hope, in this event, that they have not chosen one of those young people who do everything flippantly; I know however that you would make a point of putting everything back on the right course, etc., doing the ungrateful work without worrying about what people said about you etc., etc." He went on for eight pages.

Boris thought at first that the shock undergone by Thomas had damaged his reason, but he picked up the letter again with annoyance replacing pity; he did not finish reading it a second time and, little by little, a kind of remorse penetrated his spirit: was he not himself one of the young scatterbrains about whom Thomas was talking and was he not only too disposed to agree with their sarcasms? The letter seemed quite definitely to contain a number of precise reproaches, as if his colleague knew about his desertion.

In any case, if he had nothing better to do, he could always return to the factory.

Towards the evening he started to clean up his room, the drawers in particular, which contained all kinds of papers and small objects in great disorder.

Above all there were postcards sent by people lost to sight a long time since and alluding to forgotten events. He also found, among the tourist prospectuses, indefinable fragments which must be souvenirs, but he did not know what they were souvenirs of: petals of flowers made unrecognizable by time, ordinary-looking stones without lustre and coming from God knows where, a dried starfish, a little ring of grey metal too narrow to have ever been a ring.

Soon there was a large pile of this flotsam in the middle of the room, and Boris asked himself what he was going to do with it; he looked at it without sadness or any other emotion; he would simply have liked to know how many years of his life it represented; he vaguely tried to calculate, but his points of reference lacked precision, and in any case it was of no importance.

He sat on the bed and plunged his arms into the pile, pulling out a random page, reading a line, looking for an instant at a picture: in essence it was like this that he had lived. The little ring fell into his hand again; it was little worn, as if a tiny finger had worn it for some time, but then it was probably not a ring at all; he remembered nothing about it.

He thought of Laura, who always reproached him for his lack of memory: she often became angry about little things which he admitted not remembering.

A street-cleaner was nonchalantly sweeping up the leaves into a heap, but while he was collecting one another escaped him and others still were falling from the trees; Boris raised his eyes towards the bare branches: there were enough left for several days, and then the little electric carts would come to tidy up for good; a pavement was not made to be blocked by leaves. He picked one up distractedly and as quickly threw it away; it drew two or three circles in the air before touching the ground. What would he do with all this pile? The reason he was hesitating to get rid of it all was that he possessed nothing else.

He picked up a new page and read a few more phrases; this time there was a short flash of meaning: a young woman whom he had once met during a seaside holiday… It was a long time ago. The last shelf at the top of the cupboard was almost empty, he climbed onto a chair and started to pile up the jumble.

Towards the end of the month of September the King fell ill and Boris, like his fellow citizens, was able to follow in the press, along with other various news items, the progress of his health. It did not seem to be very serious: a simple fever which kept him in his room, which was significant in that it prevented him from playing his role in the official events.

The news was announced on a Saturday morning: mildly ill, the sovereign was unable to preside, the next day, over the reconsecration of the Cathedral of Retz, of which the restoration works had just been completed.

The Church, which was counting on this important ceremony to help its electoral propaganda, had announced some time previously an extravagant programme for the day: a large fleet of coaches was to carry thirty thousand of the faithful to hear the royal address and receive the blessing of the clergy; later, after various speeches, the festivities would continue until evening, and nothing had been spared to make the event a public success as well as a political demonstration.

Looking at things objectively, the matter did not justify all the fuss, because the old cathedral had not been in such a bad state: only superficial damage prevented it from being used for services; doors that had been pulled off, broken windows, dilapidated panelling inside, all easily conferred the appearance of a ruin, while the edifice was actually solidly standing. This was indeed why it had been decided to use it as an illustration of the famous "public works" campaign, along with the fact that it was so near to the capital. Hundreds of workers supplied with first-class materials had replaced the local mason who, with two helpers, had for years carried out a slow and sporadic task; in less than a month everything was finished. A few carping art critics had of course tried to create a scandal, but the Church considered the result to be admirable.

The King's dropping out, which had occurred at such an inconvenient time, produced a certain wavering in the press: for some, the ceremony should go ahead as planned, whether or not the King could be present; others estimated that his illness was serious enough for the pomp to be suppressed as a sign of national sympathy; and then others thought that the inauguration should purely and simply be delayed until later on. It was only during the evening that the radio gave the official story: indeed, the King was not getting better, but he had personally requested, given the importance of the occasion, that it should be celebrated without delay with all the appropriate pomp and circumstance; but perhaps the feast could be shortened a little given the situation.

Unfortunately, even among those who were interested in this information, there remained a doubt, given the nature of those commentators who had during the day given opposite opinions.

On Sunday, early in the morning, it began to rain, contrary to all expectation, and it was still raining at midday, with the sky heavy enough to leave little hope of improvement. At one o'clock, the vehicles did not even pick up a thousand people; even among the officials there were ministers missing who were afraid of catching cold. The speeches took place according to plan on the square in front of the basilica; the rain was not very heavy, but most of the speeches were rushed through in haste and everyone took refuge as quickly as possible inside the cathedral. There, a disagreeable surprise was to douse the optimism of even the most devoted: almost as much water was falling there as outside; small but numerous leaks in the material, which had not been noticed in the rush of completing the restorations, now revealed themselves in practice. It was probably not too big a problem, but the impression produced was disastrous. Jokes soon livened up the general consternation and, from the moment that people let themselves openly criticize the roofing, they might just as well attack the rest of the repairs: the carved ornaments were far from the quality of the originals, the stained-glass windows shouted out their bad taste, the paintings seemed suspiciously mass-produced.

Boris, who had not left the town, noticed the change of atmosphere in the embarrassed or sometimes overtly ironical articles in the evening papers. He wandered through the streets, among the leaves fallen from the plane trees which glistened on the oily ground; the water revived their green lustre, yellow and rusty with a fragile brilliance, while the rest of the scenery was grey and colourless.

He picked up a leaf and followed, for the length of its indentations, the sand which bordered the sea; the water was so calm that one could hear the sound of the drops hitting the surface. Round about one could not see very far: there was already not enough light.

At nightfall, he met Laura coming back from Retz and she seemed despondent; he questioned her about her sombre expression, which he had seldom seen on her; she gave him no direct answer and went into explanations that he did not understand very well: she did not seem to hold either the monarchy or the autumn in very high esteem, and as the masses were demonstrating so little faith, other means would have to be found to convince them.

From day to day the fog seems to get thicker; already we cannot see more than a step away, or else at times there is a gap of a few metres in its continuity.

It is only rarely that one can ever, because of this, see anything in its entirety: through the vents of a curtain we would suddenly see the head of a sheep emerge or the edge of the sail of a windmill, but never the whole windmill or the whole sheep from its feet to its ears; and if we were to run into the branches of a bush, we would not even be able to follow it with our eyes as far as its trunk; on the contrary they would seem to us to be branches suspended in the air, floating branches of which nothing visible attaches them to the ground. Only things that are very small succeed in being totally visible, however veiled, in their entirety; the swallows from the sea, for example, are so small that sometimes we surprise one, whole, in a gap in the fog; then still it does not have the clearest contours and in any case is isolated from its context: there is no question of knowing where it comes from or where it is going, we only have the right to see the little moment of flight in this tiny moment of its life, without a past or a future. Perhaps it is flying from a roof to a rock, or else it is accomplishing a longer flight; we cannot know. And so we only have a fragmentary idea of the things that surround us.

The beaches of the west are probably immense, because we can walk for hours and hours without reaching the end, although we will only ever discover the few inches of grey lifeless sand that we tread. We do not even dare to go along the cliffs; it would be so easy in our blindness to put a foot into empty space while thinking that we were still on firm rock. Even the lower coasts are not without danger, because the humidity in the air is so great that one can walk into the water without realizing it; the thick dense fog makes the water indiscernible on contact, just as it stifles the sound and masks it from view; one by one its specific characteristics are blurred. That is when the most painful respiration that we can feel invades our lungs, and we walk backwards when we have the courage to do so...

Sometimes the men of the village have left in this way for an errand which hardly takes an hour and have never returned; but perhaps they are still wandering somewhere on the island, away from the known roads, lost in the fog and the night.

13

B ORIS OPENED THE DOOR and found himself face to face with two policemen in black uniforms and flat caps. They waited a minute, looking at him carefully, then without turning his head, the older one said to the other:

"It's him alright, without any question."

"So we take him with us," replied the younger one.

Boris asked himself if they had been there a long time, waiting on the doorstep, or if they had arrived just as he was going out. He said nothing, as the others were not speaking to him, but when he had closed the door the older made him step aside with a gesture and, having ensured that the lock was working properly, put the key in his pocket; Boris only made a mental note that he would have to ask for it back later on. All three of them descended the staircase.

Boris was a little embarrassed to have to walk past the concierge in this company; fortunately the corridors lacked light; and then he could always pretend that these men were his friends. They had been going down for some time, holding the banister because of the darkness and trying each step carefully; these were in fact not very easy: steep and irregular, worn in most places and partially broken here and there; a few of them were even missing altogether; it was necessary in that case to make a jump into the darkness, which was a considerable risk. The second policeman lost his footing and swore softly; the bag, almost as large as himself, that he carried on his back troubled him considerably; Boris was on the point of offering to help, but no one had yet spoken to him and, after all, he did not know them.

And then, after some brusque elbowing, they found themselves outside on the heathland. They paused, but did not open their mouths; the one who was carrying the bag came out last and, panting, put his burden on the ground: it was a sheath of white cloth – a sewn sheet probably – about the height of a man. Boris raised his eyes towards the crenels in the tower and saw four or five crows looking at him, their heads slightly inclined to the side; they must have been very large to be so clearly visible at that height.

"Come on," said the older of the two, "we have to go now." And he started down the path, Boris in step with him, the other following with the bag. It was hot out; turning around, Boris saw the policeman wiping his forehead underneath his cap; he was about to ask him, to get into conversation, what he was carrying that seemed to be so heavy, when the man cried out in a sullen voice: "Can't you leave him alone? What's he done to you anyway?"

The one who was walking on ahead stopped as well and sought a more amiable way to inform him: "He's a funny sort, isn't he? What can he be doing up there all day long?" Boris replied that he did not know, and they continued on their way; the young one changed his bag from one shoulder to the other, grumbling: "It's going to make a big fuss because he was foreigner; I know it's all the same to you." Soon he stopped once again, saying in an exasperated voice to Boris: "Well then, as you found it so amusing to kill him, you might as well carry him for the time being!" And he handed over his burden.

"Is that all right?" asked the older one.

"It's all right!" answered Boris, but he walked on with difficulty, doubling under the weight and stumbling over the rubble which blocked the roadway. The two policemen, walking with a lighter step, were soon up ahead. Once or twice they looked back to tell him to hurry up: they were laughing and seemed to be mocking him. The black dog, which had run off towards a rubbish heap, came back to encourage him with its barking.

Then, the policemen having disappeared behind some scaffolding, Boris stopped and, without hesitation, tipped the body with a vigorous gesture between a pile of scrap metal and an old shed of corrugated tinplate; there was a noise of collapsing metal, the dog sniffed around, then took off like an arrow in the same direction as the others. Having looked left and right to make sure that everything was all right, Boris decided to leave the place.

When he opened the door, he saw two police sergeants climbing the steps with a heavy tread; he went out and turned the key in the door; the two men continued to climb the steps slowly up to the next landing. Boris put the key back in his pocket and went down.

He saw the concierge in front of her lodge, and she greeted him with a friendly remark of which he did not quite catch the meaning; but as he had in any case recognized the word "work", he exclaimed in a tone that was at the same time contented and resigned: "One has to!" and moved towards the tram stop.

There were a lot of people as usual, labourers and office workers for the most part; some of them were wearing the green insignia of the Church. In the tram one group was talking about the failure of the previous night's ceremony, each one telling in detail the reasons he had stayed home; but one of them suddenly declared that "that's all a lot of childishness" and the others stopped, not quite sure if he was talking about the event or their excuses for not taking part.

Boris looked at the coal merchant's shop in front of which the tram had stopped: he had on display little glass bowls each containing five or six pieces of coal, exhibited like precious fruits; he knew this window display by heart, encountering it every day morning and evening, and paid it no attention. He repeated to himself mechanically the last words he had overheard: "That's all a lot of childishness," it was childishness…

And then there was a gap.

Boris came back to consciousness, ten minutes later, among the flat sombre houses of the suburbs; the first thing that his consciousness registered was the phrase: "That's all childishness," which ran several times more through his head, but he doubted that he had been repeating it all this time in this way. More and more he realized that he did not very well follow all the things that were happening around him. He felt tired; and yet he had been resting for several days.

The lugubrious façades stretched out on each side, with their windows as narrow as loopholes, where the faces behind the dirty panes grew longer, pressed against the glass between two grey hands.

As the tram slowed down to take the corner, Boris let himself slide off it without waiting for the stop; but, having badly calculated his jump, he only just missed falling flat; for a few seconds he had the painful sensation of plummeting into space, but a rush of heat went through his whole body as soon as he could regain his balance. He arrived at the big gateway at the same time as those who had waited for the stop: trying to go faster, he had gained nothing.

A new anxiety seized him: he had forgotten his pass card! He began to think as rapidly as he could during the few steps that separated him from the security point. If he stopped to go through all his pockets there was obviously a small chance that he would find the card, even though he could not remember having carried it on him during the last few days. On the other hand, if he waited too long in fruitless searching, he would soon find himself all alone under the watchful eye of the guard, thereby losing the chance of passing undetected in the throng, in the middle of the crowd which had just descended from the same tram as himself. As for the drawback to the second solution, it was quite evident: if he behaved from the beginning as if he knew he did not possess the card, he could not, once caught, show astonishment at having forgotten it through carelessness.

He was not thinking very quickly: before having taken a decision either way, he had passed through, almost without noticing; once he had arrived in the big alleyway, he hunted vaguely in his pocket: the card was there.

The odour of hot oil caught him by the throat at the threshold of the workshop; in the hall the noise of the machines was deafening. The time clock indicated eight twenty-eight, he hurried towards the time cards on the wall to take his own – eight twenty-nine – his was not in its alphabetical place, he had to look for it all over the board, but still he could not find it. In vain he went through the complete series of cards several times; as, pressed by time, he was unable to do this calmly, he kept getting the impression that he had overlooked his – eight thirty – if in less than a minute he had not found it, the clock would register his lateness. One more time he went over the list of names: Abba, Acer, Acimin... they were all in proper order, but his was not there – eight thirty-one – he went back discouraged;

Red, the student, was there looking at him, dressed in a kind of shooting outfit and holding an enormous dog by a leash. Boris was about to talk to him, in desperation, even though he had nothing to do with this section, nor with any other as far as he knew, when the young man said to him matter-of-factly:

"They took away your card because you stopped coming: they thought you were dead. Anyhow it doesn't matter: as you're here, you might as well go up."

Boris climbed the staircase. Going along the glass gallery he felt dizzy, so high did it tower over the machines below: the workshop was immense and so deep, so long that what came up was a vague and menacing rumbling sound, in a bluish light; to get over his feeling of weakness, he quickly went into his office.

The student went straight to the desk to sit down, the black dog sitting facing him in Thomas's seat; he was sitting upright on the chair, his ears nearly touching the ceiling. There was no chair for Boris, who remained standing in the angle of the door, while Red started to operate the old calculating machine at an unimaginable speed, risking bringing about its destruction; with his other hand he was lining up impressive columns of figures without ever looking at the screen of the machine. He was no doubt making errors in his calculations, perhaps even considerable errors; Boris felt a confused anger growing inside himself, of which he could not discern the exact cause, but which quickly became intolerable; he tried to interrupt with a motion of his hand. The black dog, which seemed to have grown even bigger, now leant forward across the table while opening a worried-looking mouth filled with enormous teeth. Boris withdrew his arm and simply said: "Thomas would have kicked up a huge fuss about this." Then he left.

On the other side of the door the two policemen in flat caps were waiting. He went on without fear and discovered a fairly large assembly whose faces took on a benevolent expression at his approach. There were many there he knew: Arnaud, Vincent, Maur, Guilhem, Thomas, as well as all the others. The arguments were calm and discreet; each one spoke in his turn, without standing up or raising his voice more than was necessary; a kind of clerk was writing down what seemed to be their depositions.

When Boris asked him if this was a judgement, his neighbour answered no, of course not, because no one here had the authority to sentence him. All the same they all wanted to establish premeditation; at least everything they knew about the circumstances, so they affirmed, tended to prove it: the suspicious walks, the purchase of the photograph and even a threatening phrase pronounced during the course of a meal. "It can hardly be a coincidence," they repeated one after the other; but there was, without doubt, some sympathy on their part, and they had to recognize the existence of some ambiguous circumstances.

There was a silence and the faux clerk bent over his book, raised his head; he looked around at those present and asked: "Shall I write guilty?" The others called out to each other in confusion: "No, nobody said that!"

Boris protested, for form's sake. "Yet the bag is there as proof," he said, pointing to the object which he had had so much difficulty in carrying. The witnesses leant over it, those who were too far away came up to look at it more closely. "A sack," said someone. "That doesn't prove very much," and that was the general opinion; he was advised to find some other evidence, but he knew that he had not kept anything else; for that reason he did not go on.

The older policeman touched his arm benevolently: "Very well. In that case you are free to go."

"It's been very hot this summer," said a voice in the room; it was not about him, his case had already been closed: he was innocent.

Once outside, he turned round and saw above him the high windowless wall of Unit 8; he was happy in any case to know what was behind that wall. He had suspected for a long time that it was not a real warehouse; all the same he should have looked inside a little harder, it did not seem to be quite as sombre as one might fear; what did the windows look out on?

Boris thought that he could return one day to inform himself on the subject; he quietly continued on his way across the dunes and the swamps of the town.

Late that night he received a visitor whom he took at first for a salesman. He was ready to throw him out when the unknown person claimed that he had been sent by Laura; all the same he only let him enter with misgivings, because the man did not have an honest look about him.

From his confused words Boris finally realized that the man was a canvasser for the Church, trying to buy his vote for the next elections; although he was astonished to see this custom still in force, the other openly expressed his satisfaction on the subject: ultimately the party heads had decided it was the safest method. So nothing was changed from the old system, even the amount offered, he said, had been re-established at the old level. Boris also wanted to know why the party had thought of him, especially as his name was not on the previous list; he was told that it was because he had been listed as unemployed. Their intelligence was good, unless Laura had simply given them his address. In any case their information was wrong: he had started to go to the factory again.

The canvasser did not insist; all the same he continued talking about his profession, to which he really seemed attached. Personally he had never had much confidence in the so-called innovations of the past weeks; one section of the leadership, fortunately, had always remained opposed, so much so that all the old organization had been kept in existence. It was now going back into operation, but it was hardly worthwhile, given the conditions, to call a general election again, which would be expensive and unpredictable; and all the same, according to the republican constitution, one should not have to proceed… Boris was not listening any more: he was unable to concentrate his mind on the rapid and sinuous flow of the stranger's words; feeling dizzy he had lost his footing and was soon moving, on his side, along a different curve. With the newspapers it was a different thing altogether: their chatter was just as meaningless, but the totality of the words having been arranged and put down once and for good, one did not experience the same unease.

In trying to stop the flow of his interlocutor, he found himself carried away by this conveyor belt of words, which dragged him along in a very awkward position. The September revolution had been just a sham: with the help of a few onlookers, who had mingled with the shock troops for fun or because they had nothing better to do, those on the party's books had been enough to swell the ranks of these tumultuous demonstrations, which were deceptive in their novelty, but in which the specialists had recognized their usual customers; nothing strange about that: those who sold their vote to the Church should really be thought of as sincere supporters; once the price had been fixed, there had to be after all another reason behind their choice. Things were not all that simple, especially in a republic... When the belt got to the pulley, Boris managed to disengage himself.

How relaxing were the little printed characters, ordered into columns, compared to this uninterrupted flow; and then there was the smell of ink, and the capital letters that caught the eye, and the tranquil phrases of which one could reread the parts in any order one chose, for as long as one wanted, without risk of their falling apart; instead of these fragile and temporary bunches of words coming from who knows where, which disappear bit by bit, eternal but fugitive, at once lost and irrevocable.

After the man had left, his words stayed behind him in the room, carelessly loitering, and Boris did not know how to get rid of them; at least they were easier to handle in this form.

Therefore "nothing had changed". It had rained heavily that Sunday; the climate of the country was probably too wet for its inhabitants to be interested in politics, people only had the time to worry about raincoats and hats made of waxed cloth: every other problem, next to this one, paled in significance. Laura's disillusioned demeanour could be explained by this, as well as her complaints about her fellow citizens' lack of firmness: all she could do, she would say, was to take her chances somewhere else, as there was "nothing to be done" here. Boris agreed with her on this, but she had gone on to say: "especially since the death of the King", but on this last point she seemed to him to be less convincing, the King not being dead at all.

Ultimately, the bad weather had been more crucial than his illness. But if the King was dead, nobody having been responsible, how did that help matters? (Some people had fired into the air, nobody knew who.) In any case the hereditary succession would have taken place.

At the end of a clear day, perhaps the last one, at the crossing of two main roads, flat and straight. One of them is bordered, on one side only, by spindly young poplars, thin, straight and without a single leaf. Almost exactly in line with it, a pale sun, whose rays sweep over the plain with an unsteady light, starts to disappear. The other road cuts this one at a right angle, in the middle of the rich earth freshly turned by the plough, which stretches out in all directions. One of the angles is occupied by a hangar, vast and low, made of tarred wood with a roof of new sheet metal...

"This land is not being put to good use: thousands and thousands of square kilometres are kept isolated by the bad condition or the total absence of transport links; commerce and industry cannot penetrate it, unexploited riches are being lost. Perhaps those lands are richer and vaster than we realize. It is roads that we need, they are our only hope of salvation."

A large lorry drives down the row of poplars, slows down at the crossing and stops in front of the hangar. On the side of the road a man in makeshift military outfit is sitting at a small table; two others are standing up next to him. At the back of the lorry one can see drawn faces as if harassed by fatigue and lack of sleep. A man gets down from the front, also in uniform, who approaches the table and shows a paper; the sitting man examines it a minute and stamps it, then he writes something into a register.

They have not exchanged a word; only the noise of the engine which is still running can be heard. The other, having retrieved his travel document, goes back to his lorry, which moves off as soon as he has climbed in. And immediately afterwards a second lorry, exactly like the first, with the same tense, silent faces, drives up to the same place and the same rapid and disciplined scene takes place.

A third lorry succeeds it immediately, then another, and still another, each driving, one after the other, towards the setting sun. It seems that this rhythm is accelerating because now we are deafened by the continuous movement of the convoy.

The sun has disappeared over the horizon and we can already no longer see the tired faces of the men; soon they will have to put on their lights.

14

A ROUND US THE FOG GATHERS, each day a little thicker, a little heavier, a little more impenetrable. There are no more floating lights piercing the clearings, no more grey veil where the contours lose their shape, we are now living in the middle of an opaque and continuous substance, which gradually suffocates us. We have never been so crushed under such a weight, never have we been so little able to make out what is around us; very soon, finding myself face to face with my best friend, I will no longer be able to recognize his features.

Sounds too become weaker: already the cries of the sea-gulls, which are flying invisibly over our heads, can no longer be clearly heard and come to us as if muffled by a wall of felt. Yesterday Marc called to me from a few feet away and I could not even decide where this voice came that I could barely hear: I shouted back, as hard as I could, but for several hours we had been turning in circles without being able to meet, and when we finally did meet again, by accident, we were both so tired that we no longer knew what we wanted to say to each other; we separated again immediately.

In spite of their instinct, the animals themselves lose their way: there is not a week when some of the sheep do not stray into the middle of the great swamp; sometimes in the fog one hears their sad bleatings which reply, far away and dying, to those of the flock they have left.

It is impossible to convey how oppressing this atmosphere is in the long run: these blind wanderings, these calls for help, these desperate appeals, and the eternal white night that makes us prisoners in its stew, hiding our bodies from our own sight and absorbing the sound of our words. In the end life slows down; and the air, richer in water than in oxygen, perhaps does us less good than harm.

Most of the time we stay enclosed in our homes. The humidity penetrates inside of course, and the little fire that we can get alight is incapable of burning properly; but in any case, the fog is less dense there: only a light vapour, which must be entering through the badly sealed cracks.

This confined existence, which seems to us to be the lesser evil, is certainly devoid of any appeal, because our houses are poor in the extreme; we own nothing or nearly nothing, there is no superfluous furniture or any kind of ornamentation, sometimes we even lack the most necessary things. The trees become rotten even as they grow, there is never enough wood for us to have anything more than one or two stools, perhaps a small table; so much so that all our rooms are bare and empty. However, as they are not very large either, we do not suffer much from this absence of furniture.

Our houses are also very dark as we have filled up all the openings, but the little oil lamp which never stops burning in its corner is a source of comfort to us. Obviously we cannot say that it really offers light: unless we are right up against it, we can see little more than if there was nothing; all the same, if we bring a hand close to the flame, from behind, we can manage to light our fingers well enough to distinguish their shape; it is a great comfort, in the night in which we live, to be able to look at a hand in this way. I often spend whole hours contemplating one of mine.

And then this feeble nightlight serves as a point of departure to help us find our way around the room: knowing where it is, we guide our steps as directed by it, as a boat does with a lighthouse.

Sometimes the flame trembles so much that we are afraid of putting it out by moving too close to it, but we take so many precautions that it is very rare for us to see it die altogether, even when one of us has to open his door. In our heart of hearts we often envy Alban, the blind man, who does not possess this solace; it is said that he knows his way about in the fog better than us, accustomed to depending on nothing that was visible, while we prefer our useless eyes and the wick of our little flickering lamps. We watch over it day and night and, when we wander outside, we are sustained by the knowledge that it is still burning.

All of a sudden I find myself before an obstacle that I had not seen coming. I can hardly see what it is, even though it is now right up against me; I run my hands over it, feeling it, trying to find out exactly what it is, but I cannot identify any known object in its vertical bars which seem to be round and as thick as two fingers, solid, made of metal it seems, and too close together for me to pass my finger through them. I stay there, without moving, perhaps waiting for them to disappear, and, little by little, I find myself immured in the heart of the fog.

In spite of the immense difficulty that I find in moving, I manage to turn around while there is still time.

Once again I come up against bars that block my passage and I stop, discouraged. I can no longer think of anything at all, not only can I no longer remember where I am, but the instinct of self-preservation makes me change my course once more. Overcome by the humidity, reeling with fatigue, I cannot even be certain that I am still moving at all.

At intervals that get shorter and shorter, I find my head touching an iron grille.

Where have I wandered to in this fog? In what labyrinth have I found myself? Is it only a sheep pen, or some kind of trap that I might have created myself to capture wild animals and in which, in my turn, I have let myself be taken? I can no longer remember anything. My head is filled with cotton wool, white and limp, just like that which enfeebles all my limbs.

It is probably one of those interminable head colds, so frequent in our climate, that is gathering in a heavy mass between my two eyes. I should not have left my room; but what is there to do day and night when one is not even able to fall asleep properly without the constant worry of letting the little lamp go out? The burning fish oil gives out such an acrid odour that I must have hoped, against all good sense, to find some relief outside; all I have done is to worsen, in making myself feel even more ill, the heaviness from which I am suffering and which remains our *normal* state par excellence. The lack of sleep, the unbreathable air, and certainly the poor food as well, so little varied, is the cause; it is therefore hardly reasonable to expect to escape it.

Sometimes, during our evenings together, Guilhem or Peire or another share wonderful stories of water nymphs and sirens; for a few minutes we dream of explorations, of discoveries, of escapes. But we all know that the sirens are fairy tales, just as much as the sailors' stories of finding promised lands, and that, even if such lands existed, they would no more be right for us than these would-be girls, half fish with green blood as cold as the water they inhale, who do not speak the same language as us.

Therefore we have no other hope but to finish our days alone on this poor foggy island, where we can no more expect to meet a siren than a tree or a river.

It is said that a layer of ashes covers everything, wrapping up each surface, every angle, every line like a gauze furniture cover, or rather like a grimy halo, which is uncovered by searching hands looking for a form that is finally solid. This dubious substance does not permit real contact, but only fleeting impressions, uncertainties, suspicions, which only increase the sense of taboo a little.

And it is not only the inert matter, but my body as well, that secretes and spins around itself this inexorable cocoon; soon I find myself walled into the solid mass without having even cried out. In a final wild gallop, the maddened stallions fight against the little spider that has caught them in its web; they beat on the door with all the force of their hooves. This time I shall not open it; the mocking visage hanging on the wall may well have a handsome smile, but I shall certainly answer with: "It's not me. Do not enter. It's not me." They are hammering furiously on all sides, and on the ceiling and on the windows; ready for the final struggle, I can hear the shutters closing all around me...

There is no final struggle, I shall die without zeal and without glory. The citadel where I have lived in retirement, that the sea snaps and menaces, already reels under each of my hesitant steps; and in the meantime at the summit of the tower, where the water has now reached all the cracks that appeared to be intact, I accomplish my final round and I feel the stones crumbling from the assault of the waves. It will not be a spectacular collapse: one will not see anything very remarkable, simply a falling-away, a rocking, a sinking to rest, and no one other than I will be able to comprehend the catastrophe. The sodden powder in the cannon will not be able to spray out a final salvo; I shall be dead and not even a little piece of wood will float to the surface in testimony.

The snowflakes are falling; in a moment it will all be finished. The cold is gaining ground. I still go forward over the same lunar landscape, where among the craters and ridges one comes across enormous chunks of rock that are semi-disappearing under the snow; no vegetation emerges any more from this flat dull whiteness, no path can be seen, neither before nor behind me.

No, it is not snow, it is only sand, the dust-like sand that gives way under the feet, but which the wind flattens again one way or another back to a virgin state. Others have perhaps come here, the marks of their passage erased and giving no sign of the direction in which they went; I myself no longer know from which direction I have come.

In any case it is already too dark to see anything at all; once again it is winter, our winter, where some unknown malady has tracked me down, from which, this time, I shall not have the strength to recover.

I am lying down in my room, this room in which I shall have passed, alone, the greater part of my life. The window behind me only feebly lights the room; the design of the tapestry on the farthest wall is already unclear. Soon it will be night.

All is quiet. Since the doctor, a little while ago, told me that I did not have very long to live, the globe, which for three days has been turning on the ceiling on its metal chain, suddenly stopped, and I have vainly tried to start it again. Absorbed by this occupation, I only noticed the doctor leaving the moment I heard him close the door; I had forgotten to ask him of what I was dying.

I am lying on my back, my head raised a little by the pillow, and I almost feel well, except for a slight coldness which is creeping up my legs. Not the slightest sound is coming from the street: I live in a quiet district where noise has seldom disturbed the peace. "Not very long left", what does that mean exactly? I tried to remember something, anything at all, but I barely managed to recover two or three images: the workmen were digging up the drains on the avenue; their faces grey with dust, they look into their pots which are heating up, while one of them pulls up a last little bucket of yellow sand at the end of a rope; there must be others at the bottom of the hole… And then it is at the edge of the sea, and once again, at nightfall…

A flock of sheep, immense, light and woolly, entered behind my back from the window; walking quickly, in silence, their heads lowered, they soon formed a long triangle among the cottages, pointing towards the summit of a low hill which restricted the view on the horizon.

As the first ones disappeared into the distance, others came up behind, always more numerous and more closely packed together. They huddled against each other, without however quite melting into a single mass. There was no shepherd or dog with them.

CALDER PUBLICATIONS
EDGY TITLES FROM A LEGENDARY LIST

Seven Dada Manifestos and Lampisteries
Tristan Tzara

Moderato Cantabile
Marguerite Duras

Jealousy
Alain Robbe-Grillet

The Blind Owl and Other Stories
Sadeq Hedayat

Locus Solus
Raymond Roussel

Cain's Book
Alexander Trocchi

Changing Track
Michel Butor

CALDER

www.calderpublications.com